Pontius Aquila:

Eagle of the

Republic

Michael A. Ponzio

Eric - I hope you enjoy

MAPonzio

ISBN:ISBN-10: 0692294554
ISBN-13: 978-0692294550 (MikeMarianoPonzio)

DEDICATION

When I was a young boy, my father, Joe, would read Caesar's *Gallic Wars* aloud as I sat on his lap. Ever since then, I have been fascinated by ancient history.

Dedicated to Joseph E. Ponzio

The History

The Roman historian Suetonius wrote about Julius Caesar:

Chapter LXXVIII. In one of his triumphal processions, as Caesar rode past the benches of the tribunes, he was so incensed because a member of the college, Pontius Aquila by name, did not rise, that he cried: "Come then, Aquila, take back the Republic from me, you tribune." For several days Caesar would not make a promise to anyone without adding, "That is, if Pontius Aquila will allow me."

- Suetonius, *The Lives of the Caesars, The Deified Julius*

Author's Note

In this novel, the years are designated by the system used during the Roman Republic. The republic was ruled by two elected consuls who held office for one year. A year was designated by the name of the two consuls, followed by the letters COS, an abbreviation for *consulibus*, 'while they were consuls'. If a consul served a second year, his name was followed by II.

Some Roman historians also used a year-numbering system for special anniversaries. This dating method was designated as A.U.C. from the Latin, *Ab Urbe Condita*. This was the number of years since the founding of Rome in 753 B.C.

Pontius Aquila: Eagle of the Republic, begins in 64 B.C. That year was known by ancient Romans as *L. Julius Caesar and C. Marcius Figulus COS*. The year could also be designated as 689 A.U.C.

ACKNOWLEDGMENTS

Anne Ponzio

John Burns

Sally Catlin

Didi Goodman

Frank Ponzio

Carolyn Siebert

Lisa Cooley

Nancy Oberst Soesbee

Thank you.

Credit-Cover Photo
By Giovanni Dall'Orto - Own work,
Attribution,
https://commons.wikimedia.org/w/in
dex.php?curid=16881463

CONTENTS

The World of Pontius Aquila in the year 689 A.U.C.

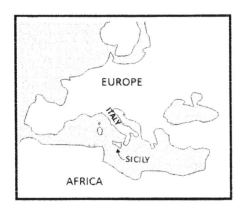

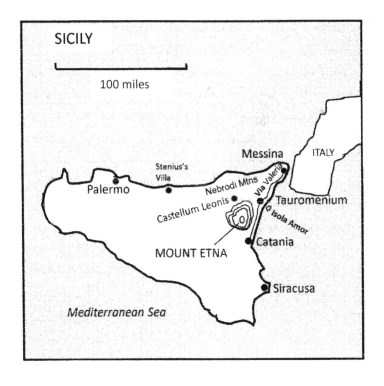

1 TAUROMENIUM

Lucius and Damianos jockeyed for position. Each pinched a glassy shard with only a quarter inch of the tip protruding. They shifted side to side, rotated, twisted, and narrowly avoided the small but dangerous blades. As the combatants gyrated, the razors scintillated in the morning sun.

Their sparring ground was a Sicilian beach covered with pebbles and cobbles, nestled in a cove, and surrounded by cliffs of black volcanic rock. Gaining traction on the stony surface was as elusive as in deep, soft sand.

Each man kept his free hand and weapon hand equal distance from the opponent to execute a common tactic: grasp and nick the opponent's arm, then exit quickly. No one wanted to maim or kill his sparring partner, but mistakes happened. Although the obsidian blades cut so cleanly they rarely left a mark after healing, Damianos sported a scar on his right cheek from a previous match.

The whirlwind of close quarter action continued. Seized wrists were pulled free, probing grasps were slapped or elbowed away, twisting, blocking, breaking free. Neither opponent could get a firm grasp. The black glass blades flashed as arms and hands feinted and blurred. A casual observer might not have even detected their weapons.

There! Lucius saw his slice to the back of Damianos's left wrist draw blood. But no! His feeling of success faded fast. In the exchange, he had also been cut. The shards were so sharp that in the heat of combat, the nicks and cuts were sometimes imperceptible.

The young men fought for entertainment and exhilaration. This was the philosophy of Lucius's teenage friends. It was a game to them, but there was blood spilled. Boasting was not tolerated.

They sparred almost naked, wearing only their loincloths, so the blood from the cuts could easily be spotted. No cuts were allowed to the neck or head and none to the groin. The winner was declared when one man cut his opponent and drew blood three times.

Each sought a weakness in his adversary's defense. Both Lucius and Damianos held their shards in their left hands, leaving their dominant hands free to grasp or to parry attacks. The incredibly sharp blades were comprised of obsidian, which in the local Greek dialect was called opsidianou. The rock had formed when the lava from the nearby volcano, Mount Etna, had cooled.

Then, suddenly, Damianos flicked up several stones with his foot, intruding Lucius's field of vision. With the distraction, Damianos thrust his heel into Lucius's abdomen, sending Lucius backwards. As he fell, Damianos followed, but abruptly stopped his assault. The tactic had backfired. During his fall, Lucius had in succession nicked Damianos's leg, sliced his right forearm and cut his hand as he tumbled back to the ground.

Unfortunately, the cut to Damianos's arm was deeper than intended. The nearest of the group quickly jumped up and wrapped Damianos's wound in strips of cloth, applying pressure to stay the blood.

Most of the young men splashed into the refreshing water of the cove and swam towards one of the black volcanic boulders, angled conveniently for them to dive from the top into the blue Ionian Sea.

As Damianos checked his bandage, Lucius slapped him on the back.

"Good one, Damianos. You would have had me on my back if I hadn't been so lucky."

Lucius returned his obsidian shard to his bulla, which hung on a cord around his neck. In his youth, this small leather sack had held a personal amulet.

"Lucius, is that why you are so skilled, because the opsidianou has been your amulet since you were a boy?"

"No, my amulet was a stone that looked like a tooth. I called it my lion's tooth, because my hometown, Castellum Leonis, was named Lion's Cliff by our Greek ancestors."

As Lucius tucked the bulla inside his tunic, he remembered the class he was to attend. By the height of the sun, he estimated it was the third hour.

"Damianos, I cannot neglect my class in Tauromenium. I just have time for a quick swim. Are you coming?"

They strapped on their sandals and ran toward the water's edge as the cobbles and pebbles slid and shifted beneath each step. They needed protection. Climbing the volcanic boulder would likely shred the bottom of bare feet. The cuts and scrapes Lucius had acquired during his sparring match burned as he dove into the salty water, but to him it was invigorating.

#

Lucius had a history of joining his friends at the beach and skipping lectures by his Greek tutor. However, today he was diligent and made it to his lesson. Class was outdoors as usual in the forum. His teacher had told him to meet at a marble plinth, which was devoid of its statue.

Lucius waited for the teacher with four other young men. Three were descendants of the Roman colonists who had migrated to Tauromenium two hundred years earlier after Rome had defeated Carthage. The other student was a Roman tourist, one of many who visited Tauromenium, which had become a holiday resort for the wealthy where consuls and patricians had built many luxurious villas. Lucius, however, was descended from Greek colonists who had founded the nearby town of Naxos generations earlier. Lucius read the engraving aloud to himself as he waited for the teacher to arrive.

"Gaius Licinius Verres."

He did not realize his tutor was standing right behind him, and was startled as the teacher spoke.

"Do you know why the statue was removed but this pedestal was left?"

"Was it stolen?"

"No, the empty plinth is a reminder of Verres, the former Roman governor of Sicily. Ten years ago, he used his position to steal valuable art and other riches from the citizens and cities of our island."

One of the students asked, "Doesn't the Senate appoint governors? Couldn't they have done something?"

"Yes, you are right. Sicilians victimized by Verres did appeal to the Roman Senate to investigate his illegal behavior, but without any results.

"Verres grew bolder. A wealthy man named Stenius, hoping to gain the governor's favor, invited Verres to vacation at his Sicilian villa while he was away traveling. Stenius returned from his travels but Verres had already departed, taking with him most of Stenius's art collection. Does anyone know what Stenius did?"

Lucius had heard of a famous lawyer called Cicero and guessed, "Stenius hired Cicero."

"Why, Lucius, there is some hope for you yet! Yes, Marcus Tullius Cicero had served as the Quaestor of Sicily and oversaw financial matters. He had demonstrated honesty and integrity in his dealings with the inhabitants. So, he was a good choice for advocate.

"This was Cicero's first important and public trial, and his case was well planned. To prepare for the trial, he traveled across Sicily collecting evidence and witnesses. Unfortunately, Verres still had loyal colleagues throughout the island so Cicero's own life was in danger during his investigations.

"His speech before the Senate was so overpowering that Verres's advocate refused to reply and recommended his client leave the country. Verres fled Rome for Gaul, never to return. Sicilians, now free of their most recent tyrant, tore down the numerous statues of Verres throughout Sicily."

Lucius was less attentive during the remaining part of the

class as they studied the works of the Sicilian poet Theocritus. The poems seemed to be unrealistic descriptions of shepherds and were too idyllic for Lucius's taste.

His attention was renewed when his teacher announced, "We are finished for the day. Now you know why we met at the plinth. As it happens, Cicero is visiting Tauromenium on holiday. I believe he is using the visit to solicit votes for the upcoming elections for consul and I am sure he will be attending the theater today. To prepare for your next lesson, attend the play at the theater this afternoon. If you are lucky, you may see Cicero at the theater."

#

The natural backdrop of the Greek amphitheater was awe-inspiring and sometimes distracting to first time playgoers. The people now assembled on this warm summer afternoon were focused on the stage in the foreground and were absorbed in the drama. As the sun sank behind the hills and its heat softened, Lucius could not take his eyes off a beautiful young Roman woman who sat with her wealthy family. He noted she was not watching the play, but was gazing off into the distance.

He also appreciated the beautiful landscape and thought that the original architects of the theater had positioned it well to frame the majestic Mount Etna. He looked across the panorama, imagining that the young woman was probably enthralled by the incredible and breathtaking magnificence of its colors, shapes, and depth. The scene was highlighted with a multitude of blues.

Everything—the sea, the forest, and the sky—existed to embellish Mount Etna. Today, his mind processed and critiqued the scene as shapes and colors, rather than as real images such as trees and mountains. The dark green of the vegetation and trees in the foreground faded into blue-green forests that climbed

Mount Etna in the distance.

A rocky coastline framed the east side of the setting and curved in alternate directions like waves in the sea itself as it receded in the distance. Aquamarine shades varied across the surface of the Ionian Sea, turning into the dark purples of the deep.

A dark blue band of thick pine forest collared the blazing white pyramid of Etna's snow cap. Above was a cerulean sky. Blue was everywhere: in the folds and valleys of the forest and the shadows of the whitecap. The color gave the observer a sensation of grandeur and mystery.

Lucius daydreamed and imagined himself with this intriguing young woman. He wished she could be with him on Etna, hiking through the dark, mysterious pine forest. He would be her handsome shepherd. She would be lost and need his help. They would drink sweet Falernian wine chilled in the snow bank and keep each other warm.

He recalled one of his tutor's lessons earlier in the day on the works of Theocritus, a Greek poet who had lived hundreds of years before in Syracuse on the coast south of Mount Etna:

> *O Aetna, mother mine! A grotto fair,*
> *Scooped in the rocks, have I: and these I keep*
> *All that in dreams men picture! Treasured there*
> *Are multitudes of she-goats and of sheep,*
> *Swathed in whose wool from top to toe I sleep.*
> *And storm and sunshine, I disdain them each.*

Lucius assumed the young woman that held his fascination was a Roman patrician visiting Tauromenium on vacation. Tauromenium, along with several other select Sicilian cities, had special status and was not treated as a conquered city but as an ally of Rome. The Roman colonists as well as the ethnic Greek descendants of these towns had the privilege of Roman citizenship.

Lucius's responsibilities intruded into his fantasy of the young woman. *What I am really going to do with these studies? Mother and Father sent me here to be educated. They gave up on me being a farmer like Father back in Leonis, and I know I should be disciplined, but I can't just sit around and study all the time when there are sweet young girls like her. She looks like a Roman—she's not as dark, nor as Greek looking as a Sicilian. Her hair is the color of honey. That intrigues me.*

Yet, what am I thinking? I haven't been able to entice any of the patrician girls, although I have tried. Besides, they are inexperienced and haughty and not as fun as the plebeian girls. All the attractive plebeian girls in town know me; not that they aren't fun, but I am looking for 'higher class pleasures.'

A hot flash of shock and anxiety ran through Lucius. He realized this attractive woman was in the party who accompanied Marcus Tullius Cicero. Lucius broke off his stare when she discovered his intent gaze, and looked directly at him. He averted making eye contact, but sensed she was appraising him. Lucius had dark curly hair that covered his ears and neck, dark eyes, and an olive complexion. In the contemporary Roman style, he was clean shaven. Average in height and compactly built, the nineteen-year-old had inherited a muscular frame, accentuated by his years of labor on his family's farm in the Anius Valley below Castellum Leonis.

The surrounding spectators were all absorbed by the play. Lucius glanced at her again several more times and noticed the young woman would not make eye contact longer than the blink of an eye. As the last act of the play ended in a climax, he grew discouraged, left his seat, and made his way to the back of the theater.

As Lucius exited the amphitheater, the audience followed and joined the slaves and vendors crowded outside. Lucius thought many of the slave girls were pretty, and he was well known among them in town. As he passed through the crowd, he smiled at a few girls he knew as they waited in the throng. Then he saw the beautiful girl of his fantasy mingling with her family. She drifted away from them to speak with a group of slaves. He hesitated, but then changed his mind and vaulted over a wall to avoid the crowd. Lucius headed to the sea along a narrow path and patted the coins in the bag secured under his tunic. There were several Roman naval galleys coming in toward the coast, and he hurried his pace.

Lucius became impatient behind the slower pedestrians in front of him, and he began taking short cuts between the switchbacks on the steep path. After descending several hundred feet, he crossed the beach where he and Damianos had sparred that morning. He then continued along a narrow strip of ground that led to Insula Amor.

Several hundred yards on his left jutting into the sea was a rocky promontory, which contained the legendary Cave of Odysseus. On his right were the cliffs of Cape Tauromenium. Straight ahead was a small island at the center of the bay formed by the two promontories.

The island was a single hill covered with lush vegetation and topped by a small columned Greek temple. Splashing on the black volcanic shore were the aquamarine waters of the Ionian Sea. Huge boulders, some large enough to be tiny islands themselves, protruded out of the sea and dotted the surface waters of the large cove.

As he approached Insula Amor, Lucius recalled what he had read in his studies of *The Odyssey*. The Sirens, beautiful women of the epic poem, would stand atop the island and chant an irresistible chorus to the passing sailors. The songs of the Sirens would steer the sailors' ships to crash onto the rocks. According to legend, the rocks had been thrown by Cyclops to sink Odysseus's ships.

Lucius saw his friends from Tauromenium diving into the water from atop one of Cyclops's islets, a common diversion for the young men. Their bodies barely missed the sharp rocks as they knifed into the sea. *I should join them! No, the sailors will get there before me.* He proceeded to the temple on Insula Amor while it was still light.

The priestess proceeded with her ritual.

"Are you ready to experience the love of Venus?"

Lucius sat on a stone bench in the small courtyard to await his chaperone to the temple.

"Yes, Holy Mother."

Two young girls, daughters of the priestesses, carried out a cup of wine, a bowl of bread, and a pitcher of seawater.

"How do you want your wine?"

As he held the cup, he hesitated, knowing the wine would be sour. Spoiled by his father's pleasing wines made from grapes grown in the rich volcanic soil, Lucius took a small sip and grimaced.

The girl with the pitcher leaned forward to add the seawater to the wine and dilute the sour taste.

"How much do you want?"

Before she could pour, Lucius moved his cup away from the pitcher and said, "Tostus."

The girl selected a piece of bread from the bowl and held it over the flames of one of the torches lining the courtyard. She handed the blackened bread to Lucius, who stirred it into the wine. He took small sips between stirring, until the sourness decreased. Lucius didn't need the wine to prepare him. He was ready to make love at any time.

#

It was almost dark as Lucius and a dozen friends sat outside the island temple passing around a wineskin. Looking across the small cove he saw the girl from the theater wander out onto the beach. She appeared to be stimulated by everything at once as she looked about, spinning in circles with arms wide out, mussing her hair to fly in the cool breeze, peering at the pebbles crunching beneath her feet, and dancing with the waves lapping along the shore. The bushes along the trail had torn her dress and her appearance had been transformed from a young elegantly dressed woman at the theater to that of a disheveled fisherman's daughter.

Sailors had pulled up two small galleys onto the beach and were gathered around a campfire drinking their sour wine. The emergence of the young woman on the beach attracted their whistles and hoots. When Lucius saw several sailors approach her, he mustered his friends to help him intervene. As the sailors approached her, she snapped out of her reverie and fled toward the lights of the temple. She screamed when the sailors caught up to her and began to drag her back toward their campfire. Lucius's vehement outcry penetrated the noisy commotion.

"Let her go!"

The sailors stopped, not because they respected the command, but because they were incredulous that anyone would be so stupid as to tell them what to do.

Several of the sailors pulled out their daggers, a pretense that was more of a threat than an immediate attack. The men with Lucius spread out behind him, none armed with knives like the sailors, but their hidden opsidianou razors were within easy reach. *My friends must think I was foolish to speak out, but I am one of them and this is our beach.*

"Of course, young noble, as you command," a sailor responded. He turned away, pulling the young woman toward their camp, "Go back to your stinking fishing hut. We found her first."

Lucius spoke in the sophisticated Latin which his teacher had taught him.

"You don't know who you are threatening. She is a patrician's daughter."

The sailors stopped again, this time to release a chorus of laughter, as the self-appointed spokesman for the sailors answered, "Yeah, pretty boy, and you, Apollo, are here to rescue her!"

Lucius persisted.

"Look at her gold ring, which by law is allowed to be worn only by patricians. Would a prostitute or a fisherman's daughter have such a ring, let alone be so brainless to wear it alone on the beach?"

This commanded their attention. The sailors stepped back

and examined the young woman. They looked at her soft hands, which were not those of a working woman. One sailor still refused to accept the evidence and asked, "What patrician family does she belong to, then?"

Lucius did not hesitate, knowing they would recognize a well-known hero of Sicily. He announced, "She is the daughter of Cicero."

Lucius noticed that none of the sailors wore the iron ring allowed only to Roman male citizens. He held up his left hand, "And I am the citizen sent by her father to bring back his spoiled runaway daughter."

The sailors groaned in unison but released her to Lucius. As they withdrew to their boats, Lucius's friends stood quietly and watched, staying long enough to make sure the sailors were not going to change their minds.

The frightened young woman sought Lucius's hand and with a shaky voice said, "Thank you. Thank you. Uh, uh, my name is Tullia."

She accompanied Lucius and his friends as they moved toward the bluffs above the beach. She followed Lucius closely and glanced back at the sailors, but they were retreating to their camp. Lucius's comrades congratulated him on his clever use of persuasion and his fine prize as they departed to continue their partying.

The trail up the cliff was too treacherous to ascend in the dark by starlight alone. Lucius collected driftwood and started a small fire to temper the cooling air. He and Tullia both sat silently watching the flames.

Lucius ordinarily wasted no time with women, but now he

only stared at the fire. *You've got what you have been looking for, a beautiful patrician girl. This is what you wanted! Why are you waiting?*

Tullia broke the silence. "I saw you watching me at the theater. Have you nothing to say? Don't you think I am attractive?"

Lucius had never been shy, and normally he would have been thoroughly aroused by now, but something inside him held him back. Oddly, he felt awkward and said, "My name is Lucius, I'm from Castellum Leonis. Are you visiting from Rome?"

"Where is your romance, boy? Theocritus was a Sicilian and a romantic. He wrote these lines just for me: 'Turn, magic wheel, draw homeward him I love. May Aphrodite whirl him to my door!'" She continued her salvo, "You are supposed to sweep me into your arms and ravish me. Am I not desirable?"

Lucius started to answer, but she cut him off.

"Do what you want with me! It doesn't matter now, I have ruined myself, and my parents will disown me after what I have done. It's just, it's just . . ."

She continued as she began to sob, "I have no freedom, no choices! I can't do anything that's interesting or exciting. I am like a slave. They have betrothed me to Calpurnius Piso to augment their political ties. Then I'll be some old man's slave. I've seen what has happened to my friends. You should be a girl. Try experiencing what it is like to be a slave. No one loves you for who you are, just for what they can do with you."

Tullia suddenly launched herself at him, wrapped both arms around him, and pushed him onto his back. She lay on top of him and fervently kissed him. The feel of her body on his aroused him and he embraced her, enjoying the contact along the entire length of his body. However, her tears and her torment stopped him from returning her kisses. She eventually quieted, and they lay there without speaking for what seemed forever, keeping each other warm. Wrapped together, they both fell asleep.

They awoke at sunrise, not strangers, but as partners who had undergone a surreal experience outside of their ordinary lives. The beach was empty of people, including sailors and fishermen now out to sea. Lucius sat up and noted Tullia's beautiful green eyes as they sparkled in the daylight.

"Do you want breakfast, after an adventure?"

She nodded, still half-asleep and disoriented, as if she could not determine where she was. Lucius took her hand and led her across the pebble-strewn spit that connected to Insula Amor.

He turned to face her and said, "Last night you said you had no fun or freedom. What would you like to do, dive off the rocks or swim around the island?"

She did not answer.

"You can swim, right?"

"Of course I can!" She dropped her tattered dress and ran into the water.

Lucius admired her trim body as she splashed into the water. Her muscular legs and firm bottom surprised him. *And I thought wealthy people got fat as they sat all day being served by slaves.* He pulled his tunic over his head and dashed into the water after her.

As Lucius ran into the water, Tullia turned around to watch him. He caught a glimpse of her small, beautiful breasts before she slipped into the water. She laughed as she said, "You *are* my

Apollo! Where did you get all those muscles?"

Lucius caught up and then led the way, fighting the eddies and swells to avoid being pushed onto the sharp rocks. They circled the island during a bracing twenty-minute swim and arrived at the pebble shore ten feet from the start of their swim on the opposite edge of the narrow spit.

As they rested on the beach, Lucius noticed redness and swelling on Tullia's legs and arms.

"It looks like the jellyfish got you." He looked at his own legs. "We both got stung."

Tullia smiled.

"It was so bracing! The swim, even the stings, made me feel more alive. Thank you for last night . . . thank you—for everything."

Girls have thanked me for a romantic night, but not the kind we had last night. This girl, this attractive young woman, seems like she could be a friend, not just a lover.

She broke his reverie.

"What about the breakfast you mentioned?"

Lucius jumped up. "Wait here, I'll be right back." He swam out into the cove where he knew there were conchs, dove to the bottom, and retrieved a pair within a few minutes.

He pressed one conch shell firmly on the ground and struck its spire with the other shell several times. After he punched out a small hole, he inserted his opsidianou shard and cut the denizen free from its shell. No longer attached, the sea snail began to slip out of its shell, and Lucius pulled it out.

"Will we eat it raw?" Tullia asked, her look more inquisitive than disgusted.

"We could, but see those two fishermen that just arrived on the beach? They have started a fire for their meal. We'll share with them."

They ate the grilled conch with bread and wine shared by the fishermen. Then Lucius surprised himself and Tullia even more. Her quote of poetry the previous night had reminded him of his lesson on Theocritus. He recited a verse by the author without an introduction:

> *I gave his mate a goodly spiral-shell*
> *We stalked its inmate on the Icarian rocks.*
> *And ate him, parted fivefold among five.*
> *He blew forthwith the trumpet on his shell.*

At this Lucius stood and sounded a loud blast from the conch shell.

"The verse was exquisite!" Tullia said as she shed tears of joy. "And blowing Triton's Horn was an artistic finish."

Lucius hugged Tullia, held her hand, and protectively led her up the trail to Tauromenium. After negotiating the steep climb to the town, they walked across the Forum, quiet and empty in the early hours except for farmers setting up their stalls of fruit and vegetables.

Tullia broke the silence.

"I am still thinking how clever you were with those men, convincing them I was a patrician."

"You mean you are not a patrician?"

"No, but of course my mother's family is very wealthy. I

know that's not why my father married her, but it helps with his political ambitions."

"Let me guess. Your father is a Knight, of the Equestrian order? Your mother's family is also Equestrian?"

"Yes, but as famous as my father is, common people would think he was a patrician anyway, so your trick worked."

"My tutor said Equestrians have served as officers in the army and have filled the administrative duties of the government all over the world. Ummm . . . that makes sense; just yesterday your father was the subject of the lecture in class. He was a respected administrator in Sicily." Lucius paused and then took hold of her left hand as he looked at the gold ring. "But what about your ring?"

"You mean how can I wear a gold ring since I am not a patrician? That used to be a law, but nobody pays any attention anymore. Anyone with money can wear a gold ring. Maybe an older patrician would be angry if he saw it, but no one would do anything about it."

Tullia led Lucius along the Via Valeria to her uncle's villa. Cicero appeared at the front gate with his wife Terentia, both looking tired as if they were up all night. They appeared more worried than angry. Lucius let go of Tullia's hand and stopped short as she went to stand before her parents. As Cicero hugged his daughter, he looked over her shoulder. Lucius's and Cicero's eyes met, both exploring. Lucius's tutor had told him a popular tale that Cicero could sense honesty in his client's eyes. When Cicero detected an immoral motive, he would not represent the person in court. *What does Cicero see in my eyes?*

#

Several days later, Cicero addressed Lucius.

"Tullia told me everything. She will be reprimanded, of course, but she has always been free-spirited. I respect a man who uses his intellect instead of brute force. I have a place for someone with your potential. You showed great discipline and maturity in resisting my daughter, considering the circumstances. With the proper training, you could become a great attorney. Besides, I am indebted to you. Are you interested in being my apprentice and training to become an advocate? There is a lot of work to be done in Rome and not enough men with integrity."

Lucius was ecstatic. *No farming! I am going to Rome—the center of the world!*

#

Anticipating Lucius's departure, his family was subdued. Although he had been a day's walk away in Tauromenium, they had seen little of him the last two years. They knew his move to Rome could be a final separation. When Cicero, his wife, and Tullia indicated they wanted to meet Lucius's family, the Pontii insisted they come to their home and enjoy a meal in Castellum Leonis.

The weather was pleasant and sunny for the noontime feast. Tables were set up outside where the family and guests enjoyed food and company. After the meal, Cicero complimented Lucius and his father, Marianus, and held up his cup of wine.

"Sir, this is excellent red wine. Its aroma and palette is familiar. I have tasted it recently, in fact . . . in Tauromenium."

Marianus tried to sound casual as he held both arms out as if to embrace the surrounding farmstead.

"We grow some of the best grapes in Sicily on the vines that surround us. But Procopius, my friend and colleague, an expert vintner, is my mentor in winemaking."

Lucius kept silent. He was concerned that Cicero would ask if his father was selling the wine. It was how his father made cash, some of which educated him in Tauromenium.

It was an outrageous and tragically common practice for large Roman landowners to obtain the most productive lands in Sicily, either legally or illegally. If this were to happen, his family would end up as virtual slaves, still working their former land, but with the profits going to a rich Roman patrician. So far, his father and his ancestors had kept a good balance. Although they were successful and produced more than they needed, the family cleverly used middle agents to distribute their products. They were trying to stay unnoticed.

Cicero paused as if he was preparing his next sentence. Lucius and Marianus glanced at each other with apprehension.

"My sister lives in Tauromenium. Lucius has been to her house and can tell you where she lives. Contact her if you need any help at all distributing this wonderful wine. I will leave word for her to be discreet. Come to think of it, I may know of some connections for you in Italy. Do you have relatives in Italy? I frequently visit my good friend Pontius Gaius at his villa in Trebula, north of Neapolis. Also, I know of a wine merchant named Pontius Arenus who lives in Rome."

Marianus hesitated in thought, curling his lower lip. "According to our family folklore, many generations ago our ancestors migrated from Greece across the sea to Sicily. Then, a young man of the Pontius clan who apparently was still restless departed for Italy. So, we could be related to the Italian Pontii."

Cicero smiled.

"A proud history! Your family's Greek heritage has enriched Sicily, and now combined with Roman ideals, has created the best culture.

"For generations my clan has lived in Rome, but we may be related to the ancient Etruscans. I had an ancestor who was a farmer who grew ciceri, chickpeas. In addition, he had a large nose with a funny cleft on the tip that looked like a big chickpea. So, it was unavoidable he was dubbed with the cognomen Cicero. The name has been passed on through generations. But I hope no one thinks that I am a chickpea!"

The men burst out laughing.

Lucius's confidence soared. *This chance encounter with Tullia will benefit my family, not just me. With Cicero defending us, no one will be able to touch our family's land now. Cicero was discreet after his initial blunder about our wine. Mother was right. She always said "It's not what you know, it's who you know."*

Lucius and his father left the others with their wine and conversations. They walked to the Lion's Cliff, the highest point in town and the site of the ancient acropolis fortified by the original Greek settlers.

As they both gazed down the valley, Lucius's father gestured with his hand across the green landscape.

"Lucius, this is all I need or ever wanted, but I know you are restless. I am certain you will find what you need in Rome."

He held up his left hand to show Lucius the gold ring alongside his iron citizen ring. Mounted on the gold ring was a single green garnet. Its sparkles reminded Lucius of the brisk water around Insula Amor.

"Cicero's comment about a Pontius in Italy was a strange coincidence. There is more to the legend. My father told me these details when he gave me this ring. Hundreds of years ago, our ancestors came from Greece, settled the town of Naxos, and named this island Trinacria. Among the colonists were two brothers. The brothers had identical rings. This ring is one of them. One brother stayed in Sicily and the other went on to Italy, maybe Rome, I don't know.

"I have asked Romans about the green garnet. They say they have only seen red garnets. But, I did learn from sailors that green garnets are found north of the Euxinus Pontus, a great inland sea."

"Father, Greeks have lived all along the shores of Euxinus Pontus for as long as anyone knows. Are these clues to a puzzle?" Never interested in family history before, Lucius asked, "Do you know the names of the brothers?"

"No, but they were probably Greek like the other colonists."

"Although Pontius is not a Greek name, it is intriguing that the green garnet is from across the Pontus Euxinus, as our ancestors were *from across the sea*. And it is interesting that Pontus and Pontius are similar," Lucius said.

His father frowned.

"Son, why haven't we had these kinds of conversations before? You are the most educated and the most proficient in Latin and Greek in the family. And I thought all you did was chase girls, but I guess you must have picked up some education in Tauromenium."

Lucius's father continued, "Whatever Greek form it was, Pontios, Pontias, Pontus, I am sure the family name has been

Latinized. It's been hundreds of years since Sicily became a Roman province. You know, Son, we consider ourselves Greek, speak Greek first and Latin second. The Romans have done much harm to Sicily and have exploited it for grain and to build their villas, but overall it has been good, at least for our family. My ancestors were always in fear of wars, either between the Greek city-states or with the Carthaginians. Two hundred years ago, when the Tyrant of Syracuse threatened us a final time, we allied ourselves with Rome and ended up on the winning side."

His father paused and returned to his earlier subject.

"After you get established in Rome, ask Cicero about Pontius Arenus. If you meet him, see what you can discover about his family history. I will never leave Trinacria, so I am asking you to do this. I am entrusting this ring to you with the promise that you will seek out your origins."

Before this moment, Lucius had never been interested in his ancestors or history. Nevertheless, as he put on the ring, he answered, "I will, Father."

2 OSTIA-ROME

The coach rattled north on the pavement of the Via Valeria, a road built hundreds of years earlier along the east coast of Sicily. The road connected Catania and the port city of Messina, located near the northeast cape of the island. Lucius observed large ships at dock being loaded with grain as other ships waited at anchor in Messina's natural harbor. Most of the vessels were used to transport wheat to Rome to feed the city's one million inhabitants. Citizens, however, could purchase passage on the cargo ships that were outfitted with cabins. Accommodations ranged from basic to luxurious, depending on what the traveler could afford.

Lucius glanced at Tullia seated across the coach next to her mother. Tullia smiled at him, but her mother did not seem pleased. A smile was about all her mother would tolerate. Terentia had told Tullia not to be alone with Lucius ever again. In turn, Tullia had warned Lucius to be careful with his behavior as her mother did not approve of Cicero bringing him along.

They boarded a large sailing ship as slaves carried the baggage on board. Tullia's family had leased two small cabins: one for Cicero, while Tullia and her mother shared the other.

Lucius would sleep on the deck. After their ship crossed the three-mile strait separating Sicily from Italy, they slowly sailed north along the coast. They dined in elegance in the fine weather, served by their slaves on the upper deck. Lucius experienced a taste of what Tullia had meant about her family being wealthy.

For several days at sea, Lucius and Tullia sat on the deck talking, under the strict observance of Terentia. Although their conversations were innocent enough, comparing their youth and present likes and dislikes and what they wanted for the future, Terentia was always within earshot, monitoring them.

After five days of sailing, their ship arrived at Ostia, the port city that served Rome. The capital was 15 miles inland on the Tiber River. When they arrived, Lucius noted that grain ships also dominated the harbor at Ostia. The seaport's hundreds of warehouses had become an immense storage site for imported grains, wine, fish sauce, and olive oil. Scores of shipping and importing companies had their headquarters in the port. The wealthy aristocracy that had resulted drove the creation of theaters, public baths, and other municipal works in Ostia.

Cicero and Lucius leaned on the ship's rail and watched the activity of the harbor and waterfront.

"Lucius, less than ten years ago, pirates burned and plundered this city. Can you believe they could do that here, so close to Rome? Pompeius Magnus destroyed their bases and eradicated them across the Mediterranean in just three months. But look, they are not even patrolling the nearby sea. This port is still vulnerable. If I get elected, one of the first projects I will propose is to build walls around Ostia."

"And why do you want to be elected consul? You are wealthy and already have the respect of thousands."

Cicero, although never a man at a loss for words, did not answer for several seconds.

"I am certain I can govern better than those in power or those vying for power, because I am driven by patriotism for Rome, not power or wealth. The men of power want to govern as dictators. They pay the soldiers themselves, who are now professionals, rather than farmers fighting for their land. So, the legionaries are loyal to the general who hires them rather than to the Roman people. The unscrupulous generals use the legions for personal ambition. Some even threaten the Senate. But Rome is still a republic. When you reach my age, the Republic will be five hundred years old. Join me and fight to make sure you see that day."

Cicero turned to face Lucius.

"Let's see how much civics you learned in your classes in Tauromenium. For formal meetings, the lictors escort a Roman consul and carry what symbol?"

Lucius answered promptly, "The lictors carry the fasces."

"What does it represent?"

"The bundle of rods or sticks tied together represents the co-consul's authority to enforce the laws by corporal punishment. The axe in it represents capital punishment of the law."

"That is true, but the bundle can also symbolize unity among all Romans. What do the letters SPQR on the fasces stand for?"

"Senatus Populus Que Romanus, meaning 'The Senate and the People of Rome.'"

Cicero added, "So, the people are important. Rome is a

republic. In Rome, after many years of reforms, the plebeians, the lower classes, attained rights to social mobility. A law passed hundreds of years ago required that one of the two Roman consuls, the elected co-rulers, must be a plebeian. Lucius, how else do the plebeians influence the government?"

"The common people are represented by the tribunes. They are elected by plebeians and have the right to veto a law proposed by the Senate if they determine that it would be harmful to the people. The tribunes are sacrosanct, and the penalty for harming a tribune is death."

"Very good, Lucius. Tomorrow morning you will attend the reception for my clients. I am not only the patronus, the head of the Tullii family, but also the patronus to my clients, who are like a kind of clan. They support me in all my endeavors, especially those in politics. In turn I help my clients, representing their interests or even defending them in the courts as their lawyer. I am afraid there will be more clients than usual waiting to see me, considering I have been away."

After disembarking, Cicero's traveling party prepared to cover the last eighteen miles to Rome by coach. When Terentia insisted they stop by the baths in Ostia, everyone agreed. Cicero would use the opportunity to campaign for the consul election.

There were small public baths in Tauromenium, but Lucius had never attended them. As in Rome, Ostia's baths included a library, food vendors, and places for exercise. Cicero introduced Lucius as his apprentice advocate. Wrestling was a common diversion, and Cicero encouraged Lucius to wrestle with some of the other young men.

He forewarned him that it was only for sport, and especially since he was a visitor, he should not try too hard to win. Lucius did not know any of the rules of social wrestling, but he often grappled with his friends and was strong and agile. Based on Cicero's comment, he assumed the young men he would wrestle would be easy victories, but he had underestimated them. They were experienced and skilled in Greco-Roman wrestling techniques. He was challenged, but adjusted to the rules quickly and was satisfied with his efforts.

After the matches, Lucius relaxed in luxury as he soaked in the hot water and listened to Cicero and his acquaintances discuss politics. When they finally entered Rome, the sights aroused Lucius's curiosity, but he understood that his explorations would have to come later per Cicero's plan. He daydreamed about meeting Roman girls in his ventures.

#

When they arrived at the large Tullii house, Tullia was excited to show Lucius around. He noticed a small statue in a niche along the atrium wall as they entered the house.

"Tullia, does this statue represent one of your gods?"

"No, the figure is the Lars Familiaris, symbol of an ancient ancestor. He is the protecting spirit of the household. We also pray to the Roman god that is appropriate based on our needs." She paused for a second, then said, "You are educated, so you know many of our gods are the same as those among your Greek pantheon of gods and goddesses."

"Yes, but the god that is most feared and prayed to at home is Vulcan, the god of fire. It is said when Mount Etna erupts, Vulcan is forging weapons for Mars, the god of war. The mountain itself is named after Aetna, the goddess of thermal geysers. I don't pray to any of these gods, although I think Vulcan is the most interesting. Whether or not you believe in any gods, if you live on Etna, you will feel a mysterious presence. I

31

cannot identify it, but many people attribute it to the gods. My father usually gives thanks to Demeter and Dionysius for good harvests and healthy grapevines."

When they entered the courtyard at the center of the house, a young woman ran across the garden squealing Tullia's name. They hugged and rocked back and forth with joy. Except for the young woman's dark hair, they looked alike and appeared about the same age. Lucius wondered if she was Tullia's sister. He was left on his own as the girls walked arm in arm across the garden. Tullia looked back over her shoulder.

"This is Prisca, my best friend!"

Lucius was given quarters in one of the bedrooms that lined the inner portico, facing the landscaped courtyard and fountain. In the morning he was awakened by a slave who brought a bowl of water and a razor and gave him a new tunic. After he shaved and dressed, he was shown to Cicero's office, where he was preparing to receive his clients. They enjoyed grapes and fresh-baked flatbread.

Some clients visited simply to maintain their friendship and see if Cicero needed any of their services. Many appealed to Cicero for help. Most of the clients requested some type of monetary loan. Cicero did not deny anyone, but sometimes would grant lower amounts than requested. However, when one client asked for a loan to start a business, Cicero awarded a much higher sum of money.

"Sir, why did you give that last client more money than he requested?" Lucius asked as they took a break and sipped some Vesuvian wine.

"His business venture would not survive with that little capital. He needed more to succeed. I want him to make a good profit and pay me back."

Cicero received numerous clients that day as the morning became an endless blur to Lucius. They stopped receiving clients for prandium, the midday meal. Terentia and Tullia joined them. Lucius discovered that Prisca was one of their slaves as she, along with other slaves of the household, served them. They brought plates of dark sordidus bread topped with chopped olives seasoned with vinegar, coriander seeds, cumin, fennel, and mint. A plate of sliced ewe's cheese was placed on the table for all to share. Wine diluted with water was served from a pitcher. At the end of the meal, Prisca approached, carrying a baby. She handed him to Tullia, who said, "Lucius, this is Marcus, my baby brother."

Lucius turned to Cicero and smiled.

"He looks very strong, sir." He noticed that Terentia had a disagreeable look on her face, as if no matter what Lucius did, she disapproved.

"I hope he turns out as intelligent as you, young man. After our meal, I will have a nap and when the afternoon cools, we will take a walk to the Forum. There I will show you how I campaign for consul.

"My opponent is a patrician named Lucius Sergius Catilina. His party is the Optimates, which is made up of conservative senators. Their primary objective is to restore the power of the ancient patrician families.

"My backing is from the Populares, the people's party, comprised of plebeians and equestrians. The party has been working for generations to expand voting rights throughout the Republic. For example, your fellow Sicilians' right to vote as Roman citizens is due to the party's efforts.

"Rome is not a democracy like the Greek model. It is a republic, a representative form of government, which gives a larger number of citizens the right to vote for consuls, tribunes, and other government positions."

"Today, all the people you did favors for and those who pledged favors to you, will they all vote for you?"

Cicero laughed.

"I hope so! Yes. And if I convince enough patrons, whether they are equestrians or patricians, that I am the best man, their clients and associates will vote for me as well."

"But you said the patricians will vote against the people, that they are not concerned with the plebeians' welfare."

"That is true, but that is also the irony of an elected official. To get elected, some will promise or appear to be what they are not, just to get elected. If they balance their promises just enough not to upset those who elected them, they may be elected again."

#

A month later, Marcus Tullius Cicero defeated Lucius Sergius Catilina and became co-consul with Gaius Antonius Hybrida. Cicero prepared for another morning of receiving his clients.

"Lucius, you have learned quickly about my clients. You have been at my side and they know I trust you. This will be my last day of routine reception since having been elected to Consul. My time must be with the Senate and government for the next year. In essence, all the Roman people are now my clients. I am asking you to carry on this work during my next year of service to Rome."

Terentia entered the room as Cicero smiled at her and added, "My wife is excellent at business. She is the absolute mistress of the house, oversees the education of our children, and manages the slaves. She has not attended our recent client interviews so you could freely learn the process.

"In a few months, after I establish myself in the role of Consul, you will accompany me as I represent some of our clients' property claims in court. So, with Terentia's return to the family business, this will give you time to also start your training in the legal area."

Lucius had not felt entirely confident taking up the role as patronus, and her presence inhibited him. He simply answered, "I'll do the best to serve you, sir . . . and you as well, mistress." Terentia smiled at him. *I am amazed, this is the first time she has shown approval of me!*

Cicero nodded. "That's fine, son. I can see you are a little nervous, but that is a good sign. It indicates you will not be overconfident and hence you will try harder. Remember, power can corrupt your point of view. To see the truth, you must always rein in your pride."

#

Lucius frequently accompanied Cicero at the public baths to learn the system of socialization and campaigning. Cicero insisted a good advocate needed to see and be seen by as many people as possible. As a consequence of socializing with older men for several months in Rome, Lucius had not befriended any young men his own age, and he missed the comradeship of his friends in Sicily.

Today he trekked across the city to a district he had not visited before, where the public bath's clientele were mostly plebeians, mixed with some equestrians. A patrician or two might show up during an election season. As Lucius watched several pairs of young men wrestle, he relaxed in the warm water. The hypocaust's central heating system, operated by slaves in the chambers below the baths, kept the water a comfortable temperature.

The matches seemed rougher than he had seen at the other baths with Cicero, but in the end, the attitudes and manners of the wrestlers were quite civil. He noticed one rather short, wiry individual who seemed to have great confidence and could challenge and compete with much larger opponents. During several matches, he observed that although the smaller man's opponents were not able to pin or subdue him, he could not dominate any of them either, and the matches ended in draws.

Lucius entered a few matches and when he felt warmed up, he offered a challenge to the small stranger. Early in their match, Lucius became frustrated, feeling as if he were trying to wrestle a handful of air. Every time he was close to having a hold, his elusive opponent was not there. He seemed almost to be able to expand and contract his torso just so he could avoid being pinned. Both exhausted, they ended in a draw, with Lucius still baffled about his opponent's techniques.

After a rubdown, Lucius joined the young man in the baths, as he lounged with a group of other men in their twenties carrying on a lively conversation.

Lucius learned that the dark and compact opponent he had wrestled was Philippus. He also met Egnatius, a sandy-haired fellow who was tall and lanky and spoke with an unauthentic patrician accent. Another one of Philippus's friends was Bolanus, who had long hair and a big nose, even for a Roman. Also, there was Juventius, whose Latin was laced with an unfamiliar accent, and Glabrio, who fastidiously continued to arrange his hair. Ricimer was chewing something, but not swallowing. Vulso listened, but did not talk much. They all were interested to learn that Lucius was from Sicily.

"I am also Sicilian," Philippus said. "What part of Sicily are you from?"

"The east coast. My family has a farm at Castellum Leonis in the Anius Valley."

"I've never heard of it. Of course, I don't know anything about Sicily except where I lived, right under Etna. My hometown is Catania."

"Leonis is on the other side of Etna from Catania. It is at least a five or six day trip from your hometown. I also lived in Tauromenium," Lucius said.

Philippus blurted out, "Are you rich?"

"No, I grew up on a farm. A few years ago I moved to Tauromenium and studied under a tutor, but spent most of my time on the beaches with friends."

"That's what I did. I mean, I wasn't studying, but I spent a lot of time at the beach in Catania. But instead of this civilized wrestling at the baths here in Rome, our sport was Opsidianou."

"What!?" Lucius splashed his hands on the water surface. "So, you must have sparred with glass razors?"

"Yes."

"How many nicks to win?"

"Three."

"That was my game, too, and we also named it after Vulcan's glass! I still carry mine." Lucius touched his amulet.

Philippus laughed.

"Me, too!"

Lucius was always good in groups and had a talent for telling stories and jokes. He related some adventures about his friends on the beach in Sicily, which his new acquaintances found quite entertaining.

Philippus turned the talk to more serious subjects. He nodded at his companions leaning against the sides of the pool and soaking in the water.

"Most of the boys here cannot find any paying work. Several of them have moved to the city because their families lost their small farms. We all live in decrepit apartment houses with our families. We are thinking about joining the Legions together. At least we would be in the country and get some fresh air. Have you heard about Gaius Julius Caesar? He is organizing legions to continue his campaign in Gaul."

"I heard the women in Gaul are wild and beautiful," Glabrio said blissfully.

"Golden hair . . . everywhere!" Egnatius exclaimed, as they all laughed.

"So, what do you do about finding girls here in Rome?" Lucius asked.

This quieted the young men's bawdy chatter. They looked at each other, then at Lucius, in silence, and then all burst out in laughter.

"Lucius, join us tonight and find out!" Philippus said.

#

Terentia smoothed the wrinkles as she helped Tullia try on her wedding dress, a white tunic reaching to her feet.

"You will make a beautiful bride and Piso is a handsome man. Your marriage will join two magnificent and noble families. Even the patrician families will be impressed. Just think, Tullia, your wedding day is next month! A wedding in June is good luck for the marriage."

She fastened a band of wool around Tullia's waist and tied it in a knot.

"Mother, why such a large knot? It makes my waist look big!"

"It is the knot of Hercules, the guardian of wedded life. On your wedding day, only Piso will be privileged to untie the knot."

"So much tradition! Now what are you doing?" Tullia said as her mother began to style her hair.

"Tullia, this hairstyle may only be worn on a woman's wedding day, or by vestal virgins."

"Why vestal virgins?" Tullia said.

Terentia continued to arrange Tullia's hair.

"I am so proud that you have shown discipline in keeping yourself pure. You will be rewarded with an upright and proper marriage as well as pleasing your loving father. You owe Lucius much. Is it true what you said? He did not violate you, did he?" She did not wait for an answer as she continued, "I was afraid you would naturally fall for Lucius after he came back with us. He is a desirable young man."

Tullia burst out, "Mother! You are attracted to him!"

"No, I really want him to succeed. Your father loves him like a son."

"Well, I love him, too," Tullia said.

Terentia's expression soured.

"No, not like that, but like a sister, I . . . I mean, like a brother, but my age. Someone I can talk to without worrying about what they think and knowing they will not tell secrets."

Terentia's smile returned.

"On the evening before the wedding day, you will give up your bulla to your father. The morning of the ceremony, I will dress you and fix your hair, just like this. At the ceremony Piso will give you a ring to be put on the third finger of your left hand."

"Why that finger?"

"Because a nerve runs directly from this finger to your heart," her mother said as she pointed to her wedding ring.

Tullia had accepted her duty to marry Piso. Her mother held much influence and power in their household, and this consolation would be a way for her to be free of her present status. Besides, he was handsome, although much older.

"So I will instantly fall in love with him when he slips on the ring? You do not believe that, do you, Mother?"

"Tullia, just let go and have some fun. Dream a little and

fantasize about him. Think of it as a new adventure! Imagine that you are so beautiful that you have Piso under a spell!"

Terentia stood behind Tullia as she remained seated and placed her hands gently on her daughter's shoulders. "We will have the marriage ceremony and dinner here at the house. Then there will be a procession to Piso's house. Servants will sing hymns and carry a wedding torch made from a branch of hawthorn. When we arrive at Piso's, he will lift you over the threshold as you enter your new home for the first time. There you will kindle the hearth with the marriage torch."

"Mother, I want Prisca to be my bridesmaid."

"I am afraid a slave can't do that. It must be someone from a noble family, sweet. Now I will tell you how to ensure both of you will enjoy your wedding night."

#

Over the next months, Lucius joined his new friends in many adventurous evenings around the city. Through their network of acquaintances, they attended drinking parties, called symposiums, where they met young women. They also were invited to select parties given by wealthy patrician women who welcomed the company of young men while their husbands were overseas serving the army, in faraway provinces.

One night, most of their friends had stumbled home from a boisterous party, having consumed too much wine. Philippus and Lucius made their way in the cool air of the night to the top of the Capitoline Hill. There they lay on their backs in the grass looking up at the bright stars.

Gazing in silence for several minutes, Lucius said, "How did your group of friends get together?"

"Lucius, they are your comrades, too! I met Glabrio in the forum. He was being bullied by a gang of boys and was outnumbered. They were going to cut his long hair. I only had to show them my opsidianou blade and they ran."

Lucius laughed. "Yea, Glabrio is so worried about his hair that he uses clips and olive oil to keep it in place.

"I can't imagine how you met Vulso. He just nods so he doesn't have to talk."

"I met Vulso along with Ricimer and Egnatius in the forum. A couple of months ago, Egnatius was standing on an empty plinth and was giving an animated monologue there. There were at least 20 young men and women gathered around him as he spoke. I figured he was just another philosopher spewing nonsense. But as Glabrio and I walked by, the throng was laughing so much, I stopped to listen."

Lucius asked, "What was he talking about?"

"It *was* nonsense. But his oratory consisted of clever parodies of politicians' speeches and lifestyles. After he finished, Ricimer and I stayed and talked with him. Then we went to the baths together."

"Was Ricimer chewing his fingernails?"

"No, but I think he had a straw shoot in his mouth," Lucius chuckled.

"How about Vulso?"

"He never said anything, like always, but he just followed us to the baths and has been around ever since."

After their laughter ended. Lucius said, "It's better we are different. How boring it would be if we were all alike!

"By the way, what do the boys say about me when I am not around? Do I have an exclusive characteristic?"

"Sometimes I have heard you called 'the equite.'"

"But I'm a plebeian, just like all of us."

"Lucius, you have been adopted by an equestrian family. Your speech and education cannot be ignored. Your personality makes you a natural leader."

"Hm. So, Philippus, what is your peculiarity? 'Shorty.'"

"Those would be fighting words, coming from anybody else!"

#

Several weeks later, after another evening carousing with his friends, Lucius was too inebriated to walk in a straight line, let alone find his way home. Philippus and Glabrio delivered him to Cicero's house. The front door, made of heavy wooden planks reinforced by an iron frame, was securely locked. The entrance was guarded by a brawny male slave and a mastiff guard dog that napped in his niche near the front door. Philippus knocked on the door, and the guard opened the eye hole. He chuckled when he saw Lucius propped between two of his friends. The guard took possession of the young man, carried the dead weight over his shoulder through the house, and set him on his feet at the doorway to his room. Lucius leaned against the door without falling, which satisfied the guard, and he returned to his post.

Lucius stumbled into the dark room, pulled his tunic off over his head and fell headlong into his bed. Almost immediately, he felt warm, soft hands begin to massage his neck and back. He detected the scent of perfume. *I didn't bring home one of those girls with me, did I?* He rolled onto his back already aroused. Even in his drunken state, with his capacity as a twenty-year-old he was ready to continue his sexual adventures for the night. He lay back as his mysterious lover took control.

In the morning he awoke late, and alone, with his first hangover since his wild nights on the beaches of Sicily. Lucius was beset by his first waking thought. *Who was that last night? It seems like a dream, but it was wonderful. Why wasn't I woken this morning? I will be late receiving the clients!* He readied himself as fast as he could, but when he entered Cicero's office, Terentia was already receiving clients and conducting business as usual. Cicero was at the Senate house. Busy and involved, she glanced over at him with no expression of irritation.

After the morning clients had been seen, the midday meal was served. Tullia joined them, holding little Marcus's hand to help him walk. As Marcus was served some porridge, Terentia remarked, "I hope you had an exciting time out last night. It is only natural for a young man to have a jaunt occasionally. In the interim, you have shown quite a bit of discipline."

Terentia's frankness embarrassed Lucius, so he continued to eat without engaging her. This was the first time Terentia had been pleasant to him since he had joined their household. Tullia, however, was sullen. At her mother's comment, she had looked up and seemed edgy. Lucius felt jittery. He broke the silence.

"Months ago, I met some young men at the baths. Plebeians and full of wild energy. They are from good families who became indebted and lost their farms in Latium. Now they barely survive in the city."

Terentia answered, "Why don't you ask them to visit as potential clients? They can help us and vice versa. I was curious, though, you attend all these symposiums around town, but it seems you have not adopted the latest fashions, almost as if your comrades' party group has established their own strange style of dressing."

"I have joined my friends in wearing casual dress, to be one of them. I do not think they can afford to stay up with the newest fashion."

She will believe that, but the truth is I have adopted the group's tendencies, which is a preference to anti-fashion. Whatever the latest style is, we will be sure we do not follow it. How strange—Terentia has never talked to me this long before without some sarcastic remark. Perhaps she is not so bad after all.

That observation led to an unsettling notion. *Was that Terentia last night? No! No! No! I am simply suspicious because she is acting differently.*

The next day, Lucius's friends appealed to Terentia for funds to purchase equipment to enlist as legionaries in the infantry. Without armor, they would have had to sign up as auxiliaries, a position usually filled by poor enlistees who were unable to arm themselves. Terentia granted their request, but she required them to enlist before she paid for the armor. In addition, they would be asked to perform services for the Tullii clan.

#

With Cicero devoted to consular duties, Terentia mentored Lucius as he received clients. She was firm but respectful when she made suggestions. After several weeks, she was satisfied he was ready to work on his own. Terentia returned solely to manage the household and reminded Tullia she would soon have the same important responsibility after her marriage.

45

One day, Lucius finished with another client and entered the garden for a break. Terentia and Tullia sat at a table where mother was teaching daughter the accounting methods for the house. Lucius was tired. "Whew! I see the sundial shows it is now the sixth hour, so thankfully I will end today's receptions. Wasn't Cicero going to come home to prandium today and give himself some rest from his busy schedule?"

"Lucius, what timing! I am right behind you!" Cicero laughed as he unfurled his toga and handed it to a slave. Now more comfortable in only his tunic, he walked briskly from the atrium into the garden area. He went first to Tullia and gave her an affectionate hug, pecked Terentia on the cheek, and put his arm around Lucius's shoulder.

"I love the peace of home and family. Let's eat. Then, of course, I will take my afternoon nap."

Servants arrived immediately with prepared food, as if they had been waiting, and covered the table with bowls of olives, fruit, nuts, and bread. Small bowls filled with garum were placed at each of the table settings to dip bread into the spicy, fermented fish sauce.

After a relaxing meal during which Cicero refrained from talking politics, Tullia left to entertain and play with her little brother Marcus.

The doorman announced Crassus, a friend of Cicero's anxiously waiting in the atrium to see him. Terentia had a sour look on her face. Cicero called out, "Let him in! Crassus is a friend and he would not be so impolite to interrupt our prandium unless there was an emergency."

Crassus handed Cicero several scrolls. Cicero studied them.

"These letters warn of an impending massacre of senators, my co-consul Hybrida, and me, by supporters of Catilina. He is so bitter having lost the election for the second year in a row, he has ignored the results. Now he has gone so far as to try to overthrow the Roman Republic. These documents must be presented to the Senate as soon as possible.

"What timing for your education, Lucius! With this news, I will show you how to plan for emergencies. The key is to move quickly and delegate to those you trust."

Cicero shouted to the scribe in the next room, who joined them in a few moments. Cicero gave him instructions. "Return here with the doorman, the head cook, and the lead messenger as soon as possible."

The scribe hustled out of the room. Cicero said, "The doorman is the chief guard and I will instruct him to increase security and to notify the entire household we are on alert status. The head cook is an outspoken and strong-minded woman. I will direct her to make sure the slaves going to market and handling deliveries keep their ears and eyes open when they are about the city. The doorman will also tell them not to reveal any security information about our house to outside sources. I will direct the scribe to send warnings to the leaders of the Senate about the conspiracy and send a copy to Hybrida. The lead messenger will arrange for couriers to deliver the warnings today. I will also call for an emergency session of the senate at first light tomorrow morning."

Within a few minutes, the scribe returned with the designated household staff. Cicero explained the situation to the group and gave each staff member details of their responsibilities.

#

For several days Cicero was extremely busy, but he finally took time one evening to explain the situation. Terentia, Tullia, and Lucius reclined on couches while they ate a dessert of fresh fruit.

"Yesterday I presented the letters from the nobles to the members of the senate as proof that Catilina was a threat. After I read them aloud, the charges were verified by Quintus Arrius. He had witnessed Manlius, Catilina's closest supporter, mustering troops in Etruria on Catilina's behalf."

Lucius added, "I heard in the Forum yesterday that Manlius occupied Faesulae but was thwarted in his attempt to seize Praeneste. Of course! That is why Catilina took his army and headed for Etruria."

Cicero looked at Lucius.

"Yes, not to stop Manlius, but to join him and prepare to march on Rome with his army."

Terentia broke in, "I am more worried about the plans to assassinate you."

Tullia promptly sat up on the edge of her couch. "Father!"

Cicero sat down next to Tullia and put his arm around her.

"My dear Tullia, do not worry. I have a plan as well. Lucius, apparently your friends are getting well-known. You must have been at the party at Manlius's house? It seems with Manlius out of town, his mistress Fulvia had a symposium. Fulvia warned me of the assassination threat and told me of your visit. I recommend that you call on her again!"

Tullia's faced turned red, as Cicero continued.

"We must keep the house well-fortified the next few days. I will require the help of your comrades to identify potential assassins on the street. I could fill the streets with legionaries, but that would just scare away the assassins to surface again later. It is no good to merely keep them out. We must capture them to discover their patrons. Lucius, you will remain in the house to ensure the safety of Terentia and Tullia."

The next morning, Lucius's friends combed the streets around Cicero's house and reported that they had detected several suspicious men trying to blend in with pedestrians and clients waiting to be seen. Over objections from Terentia, Cicero decided to allow the conspirators to lure him out. He donned armor which he wore hidden under his toga, then exited his house.

Since his election to consul, he had been accompanied by two lictors. Each lictor carried a fasces as well as being armed with a short sword. When the small entourage crossed the street, three conspirators drew their daggers and lunged at Cicero. The lictors blocked their attack and held them off with their rods. As the lictors started to draw their swords, the assassins fled.

Lucius's friends gave chase and the pursuit led them down side streets and into back alleys. Philippus, the fleetest of foot, foolishly ran ahead of the rest. For a few minutes, the group lost track of both Philippus and the assassins. As they frantically ran down a main street, Glabrio looked sideways down a dead-end alley and caught a glimpse of Philippus surrounded by the three assassins. Glabrio stopped and shouted for the others to return as he backtracked.

As he rushed into the alley, he saw Philippus spin and evade the daggers of two attackers. The third assassin was crumpled on the ground, holding his neck with both hands as blood seeped between his fingers. The two attackers again rushed Philippus. He seized the dagger hand of one attacker and slashed his wrist with an opsidianou blade to disarm him. As metal rang on stone, Philippus yanked him in front of the other opponent and used him as a shield. Philippus's friends ran down the alley toward the fight and the remaining assassin threw down his knife and surrendered.

Lucius joined them as they returned from the altercation. He slapped Philippus on the back and said,

"Opsidianou!"

#

Two of the assassins were taken into custody. The third had bled to death after he sustained a deep cut to the neck.

Several days later, Lucius began the legal defense for Philippus, who had been accused of murdering one of the conspirators. Although it appeared obvious what had happened, Lucius was finding what a political and litigious world was Rome. Lucius made a good case and explained that Philippus was a loyal client of Cicero and was simply defending him from harm.

The opposing advocate indicated that the three citizens who approached Cicero were planning to appeal to Cicero for help, and did not have associations with Catilina as accused. The advocate emphasized it was neither illegal nor unusual for citizens to carry daggers for self-defense. It appeared the trial might be a draw, even though the truth was obvious to those who had seen the event in front of Cicero's house.

Again, Fulvia came to the rescue. She seemed to want to sever her association with Manlius and Catilina's group. She testified she had heard of the conspiracy from Manlius himself and had seen him with the accused assassins. Since Manlius refused to return to the city to refute this, Philippus was acquitted.

Several days later, Cicero and Lucius stood at the Rostrum, the stage from which speeches were given to the public in the Forum. As the crowds gathered to hear Cicero, he informed Lucius of an episode at the Senate that had occurred the day before.

"Lucius, it was almost unbelievable. Catilina, acting extremely confident, returned to Rome, and sat in the Senate as if nothing had occurred. No other senator would sit near him."

"So, what did you do?"

"I gave him a chance to redeem himself. I recommended the Senate allow Catilina to voluntarily go into exile and disband his army. Catilina countered with his own speech, as if he was exempt from punishment by emphasizing his ancestry as extremely ancient and powerful. He also pointed out the lack of proof. The Senate, angry at his actions, shouted him down and he promptly fled Rome again and returned to his rebel army."

"So, will the Senate send legions to stop him?"

"Yes, now we must fight."

As a squad of legionaries escorted four men in chains to the Rostrum, Cicero gained the attention of the crowd and he pointed to the prisoners.

"These traitors were caught today trying to convince members of the Senate to side with the revolt! This is the proof justifying my actions on the Catilina conspiracy."

As Cicero continued with his speech, he emphasized that he

was on the side of the people and Catilina was not. Cicero reminded them that he had sacrificed his own popularity with certain nobles to protect the common people from Catilina's plots. He finished with an appeal for the audience's judgment.

"The law will allow me, by manifest of martial law in emergencies, to execute these men without trial. However, I have asked the Senate for their ruling. The Senate has just overwhelmingly voted to execute them immediately. Now I ask for your approval. What do you say?"

Without hesitation, voices from the crowd shouted.

"Kill them! Execute them! Do it now! Catilina will be another Sulla, destroy his army!"

#

The threat of assassination and local insurrection ended. Military action against Catilina was underway far to the north in Cisalpine Gaul and normalcy returned to Rome. Cicero arrived home from the senate house one day as his family was enjoying the midday meal in the inner courtyard. He entered the garden looking jubilant. "It's over! Catilina died fighting alongside his army, which was destroyed near Pistoia by the senatorial legions led by Hybrida. When we announced it in the Forum, people shouted that I was 'the father of the country'!"

Terentia, Tullia, and Lucius clapped with joy and Cicero's young son Marcus joined in. Cicero removed his toga and relaxed in his tunic under the warm June sun. Terentia went over the highlights of the morning's client business. Cicero sipped his wine and said, "Lucius, I am going to have to order some more amphorae of your father's excellent wine. In addition, I will find a distributor in Rome to set up an account with him."

"Husband, remember Tullia's marriage is next week. And Tullia, if you have not decided who will be your bridesmaid, I have asked for my niece to stand in. She is very beautiful."

Tullia tensed but then quickly relaxed as she responded, "Lucius will be my bridesmaid, of course. Isn't the bridesmaid usually the bride's best friend?"

"Sure, I'll do it! What color is my dress?"

Tullia added, "Mother, I have asked Procopia, one of the girls that I am tutored with, to be my bridesmaid."

"I have never met the young lady. I assume she is the daughter of M. Procopius Petrus?"

"Yes."

Terentia looked relieved as she said, "Excellent choice, Tullia."

Cicero leaned forward in his chair and said, "Lucius, you have been here for almost a year. You have developed into an effective advocate. We have discussed that the next step for your career is military service. I was in the legions for almost ten years. I did not particularly like it, but it taught me much about the world and people. Military service is essential to help you launch your political career.

"Annius Drusus Pavius, a veteran centurion who has recently recovered from injuries in the Gallic War, will lead you and your group of friends to Gaul to join Legio VI, a new legion being formed with Italians and Spaniards. In a few days, you will be fitted for your armor, and next week after Tullia's wedding, you will report for duty."

3 GAUL

Their orders were to meet Centurion Annius Drusus Pavius at dawn. He would be waiting for them at the Campus Martius, a large training field just outside the north wall of Rome. Cicero had told Lucius that Pavius was only twenty-nine but had served in the Roman heavy infantry for ten years, five of those years as a Centurion. His family was a client of Cicero's. His pledge was to prepare Lucius for the legions. They brought their armor, hobnailed military sandals, and the military kits issued at the enlistment station.

As Lucius trooped across the large meadow, events of the last few days filled his mind. *Tullia's wedding is done.* He chuckled at how she had tricked her mother. *No one noticed except her family, but Tullia had her way after all, and her friend, Prisca, was her bridesmaid. By the time her mother detected the switch she could not stop the wedding. She was trumped.*

Now his group of friends—including him they were eight—slogged through the tall grass, the lower half of their bodies becoming soaked with the morning dew. They each carried a rectangular shield made of leather and canvas stretched over a wooden frame. Their body armor consisted of curved strips of metal held together with leather thongs, worn over a woolen knee-length tunic. Each man wore an iron helmet fitted with hinged cheek pieces. A rim ran along the back of the helmet which protected the legionary's neck.

Ahead in the morning mist a lone figure was waiting for them. They stopped a few yards from the man, forming a rough semicircle around him, waiting for instructions. He said nothing and they remained silent. It was too early in the morning, even for them, to start their usual raucous behavior. Besides, they were all apprehensive about what to expect from this battle-hardened veteran. They knew better than to start any joking.

Pavius was an imposing figure. He assessed the group of young men and announced, "During our march to Gaul, you will learn that the success of the legions begins with the cohesiveness of each squad of eight men. By the time we reach Gaul, you must be physically ready and must trust each other to move as a unit. Rome does not win its battles by luck or with mercenaries, but by the discipline and hard work of its citizen soldiers."

Pavius waited. Lucius sensed in the way the centurion stood that he was waiting for one of them to show impatience, so he could make an example of him and crack him across the back with his vinewood staff. They all stood silently.

Pavius called out, "Line up, men, abreast!"

Pavius's expression was one of surprise. They did not hurry. Instead of stumbling over one another determining who was to stand where, they lined up without talking, and each held his shield against his chest. He addressed the young men.

"Have any of you served in the legions before?"

Lucius answered, "No sir."

Pavius paused, then said, "Do all of you already know each other?"

Lucius answered, "Yes sir."

"The eight of you will make up a squad of legionaries. A squad is commonly called a tent as you will all share a leather tent. You will also share a mule and eating equipment. Your tent will be one of ten tents that together make a century, which is the unit I will command when we reach camp. Six centuries form a cohort and there are ten cohorts in a legion."

Pavius looked up and down the line as he tried to size up the group. He looked at Lucius, standing on the far right.

"In this short time, I can see that you are this group's leader. The man next to you is the most fearless and the most trusted by you. One or two of the men in the middle are either less competent or their actions are of the least consequence."

He again addressed Lucius.

"Tell me your names, men. Starting with you, tell me your familiar name."

"Lucius." "Philippus." "Juventius." "Ricimer." "Egnatius." "Vulso." "Bolanus." "Glabrio."

"You, Philippus, may not pass the minimum height for the heavy infantry. I'm not certain what will happen. You can go with us to Gaul and take a chance on the Legate's decision." For an instant, Philippus started forward before he pulled back and corrected himself. Lucius was relieved Philippus kept his temper under control.

The centurion spread out his own kit, which was identical to those issued to the recruits.

"Men, form a semicircle around me, sit down, and place your kit on the ground before you.

"Your two-edged short sword is designed best to thrust, not to slash. As a backup for closer quarters, use your dagger." Pavius balanced a javelin, or pilum, holding the wooden handle made of ash as he asked, "Do any of you know why the javelin head and shaft are made of two kinds of metal?"

They were all silent until, to their surprise, Vulso answered.

"My father was in the infantry. He said the iron points were tempered but the shafts were untempered iron. When a javelin hits a target, the untempered shaft will bend on impact and thus the enemy cannot use it."

"That's correct. Excellent answer, soldier!"

"Men, also included in your kit will be a digging tool, either a spade or a pickax. You are legionaries, but you will use these tools more than your weapons, constructing the legion's defensive camps, fortifications to besiege a city, and roads."

Pavius sat down and, instead of brandishing one of the weapons, he picked up a pair of coarse stones. "I am going to show you how to make bread."

Pavius demonstrated how to grind wheat using a hand grain mill consisting of stone mortar and pestle. He then formed and baked a small flatbread that would be their food staple. Portions of vinegar were diluted with water and rationed out to the men.

After their breakfast, Pavius demonstrated how to arrange their armor, kits, and short swords into packs that they would balance over their shoulders on long wooden stakes for the march.

When everyone had his own pack ready, Pavius had three men line up in the first row, making three abreast, with Lucius in the front row. They were followed by a recruit leading the mule. The mule was followed by a second row of three men. Pavius marched in the rear with one recruit and filled him with army information. Over time, each recruit would march with Pavius in this position, to be indoctrinated.

Pavius announced, "We are going north on the Via Aurelia to Pisae and continuing on the Via Aemelia Scaura to the fortress at Mediolanum. That is where the Sixth Legion is being organized to serve in Gaul. Since you are beginners, today we will march only twenty miles. Legionaries, march!"

After several hours, the group developed a marching rhythm. The wooden stake supporting seventy pounds of equipment was soon digging into Lucius's shoulder. All Lucius could think about was how the pain increased with each step on the paved road. He tried to concentrate on other things, like counting steps until the next mile marker went by or gazing at the green hills in the distance. Pavius stopped them at five miles.

"Drink past the point you think you have satisfied your thirst. It will make a difference later."

During the second five-mile march, the local traffic, which had been mostly farmers carrying produce to Rome, became less frequent. A coach carrying civilian passengers passed them going the opposite way. Pavius did not command any of them to change formation, leaving just enough room for the two parties to pass each other. As they reached their second stop, the driver of a postal coach passed them going north and blew on a horn to warn them.

On their third stop near a village, they obtained some chickpeas and bread. As they rested, they ate and drank.

Pavius pointed to a nearby grove of trees.

"We'll collect chestnuts from those trees and then have some vinegar. Collect ten handfuls each for your meal later."

After foraging, the group sat chewing chestnuts and washed them down with the vinegar.

Glabrio said, to no one in particular, "These nuts are bitter. Chestnuts for lunch and for dinner. Maybe we will at least be able to roast the nuts later. Now that would be much better. And do I just love that sour wine!"

Most of the rest of the men were too thirsty and tired to carry on their usual banter. As Ricimer munched away with the others, he rubbed one nut on his nose. He examined the nut between rubs to see how shiny its shell had become.

"That's a shiny morsel you've got there, brother," Juventius commented.

"My grandfather used to rub chestnuts on his nose to help with aching joints and muscles. He says the chestnuts stop the soreness. Remove the nut from the cover and then rub the chestnut on your nose. The oil from your nose makes the nut a shiny souvenir. My muscles are getting sore and we've got a long way to go. You should keep one nut in your tunic and occasionally rub it on your nose," Ricimer explained.

The men's laughter was interrupted as Pavius rejoined them and thundered, "Idiots! Don't eat the chestnuts raw! Let's march!"

Late that afternoon at their last stop for the day, Pavius

instructed them how to make chestnut bread. They roasted the chestnuts and then ground them in their hand mills. They added a little water, chickpeas, and salt and mixed it together to make dough ready for the fire. They all agreed, in their exhausted state, the bread was equivalent to a feast.

Day after day, they marched; as the soreness turned to pain, and back to soreness, and finally disappeared. Their goal was Mediolanum, the capital of Cisalpine Gaul. The town was a large military outpost used as a base by Gaius Julius Caesar, the governor of the Roman provinces north of Italy. From this outpost, Caesar had crossed the Alps and conquered Transalpine Gaul.

Now in marching shape, they would train in military tactics when they arrived in Mediolanum. During the long hours of their march, Pavius made them memorize signals and commands for their squad to move as one when in marching formation and in battle.

Above the clatter of their marching footsteps, Pavius described the dimensions, configuration, and methods of construction of a standard Roman military camp. He told them the legions always built a camp each night when on campaign in enemy territory. Every time they stopped to rest, Pavius would use his vine staff to trace in the dirt the arrangement of the standard fortified camp. He showed the position where each unit of a legion would camp and the location of the gates, roads and headquarters. The recruits memorized what part of the earthen wall and ditch was their duty to construct, where to pitch their tent, and which part of the wall to defend if under attack.

They finally reached the walled city of Mediolanum. The city had recently undergone rapid growth due to the surrounding fertile agricultural area and its role as a trade center at the hub of a web of Roman roads. Adjacent to the city was the largest military camp in Italy; it was used for training and sending legions to the Gallic campaign across the Alps. It was not hard for Lucius's group to find their tent site in the Sixth Legion's camp. After Pavius had told them to which cohort they had been assigned, they knew exactly where they would be located as all camps were configured alike.

During their march north Pavius had shown them how to salute the standard, commonly called the Aquila, as they entered camp. The Aquila, a pole topped with a figure of a golden eagle, was assigned to each cohort, which consisted of 480 legionaries and to each legion, which consisted of ten cohorts. Pavius had instilled in them the importance of the Aquila. It was considered sacred and to be respected and defended at all costs.

Pavius then saluted them by thumping his right fist on his chest and voiced the familiar, "Virtus!" (Heart! Courage!) He then left for his new assignment.

The group found the correct place to pitch their tent among the orderly rows of the Sixth Legion. Their new centurion, Marius Duilius, inspected the squad's domicile, and led them to the unfinished ditch and palisade. They joined other legionaries in the backbreaking work. Working nearby was a robust legionary. His receding hair, however, made Lucius think the man was middle-aged. Lucius noted the fellow must have been working for quite a while as his tunic was grimy and full of dirt. The man worked steadily. He used his spade with determination as he excavated the ditch, piled up the dirt to form a defensive wall, and then drove wooden stakes into the dirt wall to form a palisade.

He must be a career centurion. Pavius told us it was common for lower rank officers of the legion to work with the troops. Without stopping work or looking at Lucius, the hard-working legionary said, "Decurion Pontius Lucius, Pavius told me your tent has great potential."

Lucius, taken by surprise, hesitated but squeezed out a weak, "Thank you. They are good men, sir."

The older man continued, "I know that Cicero arranged to have you join the Sixth, because his brother Quintus is the legate. You are also very fortunate to have the Centurion Primus Pilus conduct your basic training. But remember, your status here is based on your own performance, not on the influence of your relatives or allies."

They finished the fortification and Marius ordered them to wash their clothes and then go to the military baths. To all Romans, cleanliness ensured health both physically and psychologically, and whenever feasible the army also emphasized good hygiene in the field.

Lucius walked with several score of men to the baths and noticed the balding fellow who worked on the fortifications speaking to Marius. He could not hear what they were saying, except just before Marius left he saw him salute and raise his voice slightly, saying, "Yes, Proconsul."

Proconsul? Lucius was staggered. *That was Julius Caesar himself working with me! So the chatter among the soldiers is true. Caesar gains the loyalty of his men by working alongside them and eating with them. They also say he leads from the front, not the rear as most generals, and he even enters the fighting. And as he told me, he promotes his men because of skill and fighting abilities and not due to their status as nobility.*

He called me decurion. I guess I have been promoted! That makes sense. Pavius did put me in the position of leader during our march north. And he said Pavius is the Primus Pilus. So Pavius is the senior centurion, the 'First Javelin' of the whole legion and advisor to the legates and Caesar himself!

The days and weeks that followed were filled with intense training. There were long drills in full armor, usually in the maniple formation. They also drilled in lines three deep and six deep. In all formations, the legionaries practiced relieving the men in the front lines to give them rest and still maintain a strong fighting front.

Pavius had taught them to look to the Legion's Eagle standard for visual signals meant for movement of the legion. The bugles were used to signal maneuvers of the cohorts, the largest division of the legion. For smaller group movements, such as maniples, they were to watch their own centurion's helmet crest and to perform infantry maneuvers according to the pitch and pattern played out by the centurions on their high-pitched whistles.

Then there were weeks of calisthenics. They sparred and practiced battle maneuvers with wooden swords and shields heavier than the standard-issue steel gladius and scutum. The daily exercises made Lucius so tired his thoughts hardly went any deeper than anticipation of his next rest, drink or food. One evening as they soaked in the baths, tired and sore as usual, he found time to reminisce.

How did I get here? In Sicily, I tolerated the tutors, didn't study enough, but somehow absorbed a little knowledge, yet I had no real goals. Then Cicero showed up and I believed I could be someone like him. In Rome, it was like I was living two lives, one becoming an advocate, the other finding amusements with my friends.

Now I construct a ditch, suffer through another drill, and survive another sparring match. I can only endure by knowing there will be a reward soon, like a simple drink of water—it tastes like the elixir of the gods! Simple meals taste like the best prepared feasts. Then there is the pleasure of socializing with friends around a fire or at the warm baths. This is all enough, but I will miss the baths when we go north.

One evening, Lucius and his tent mates had just finished sharing a meal with the legionaries quartered in adjacent tents. Bolanus approached the group as they sat around their campfire. With him was another legionary holding a ceramic mug of dark, viscous liquid.

"Here is the pitch and pine resin to remove your beards. Who is ready to get their face ripped off?"

Philippus remarked, "I never routinely shaved. But spoiled Lucius here, he was shaved by a servant every day. Isn't that right, Lucius?"

"Or maybe pretty Tullia did it for him. We know the wealthy are always worried about looking proper according to the latest styles," Glabrio added.

"No, no, I could have had a slave help me groom every day. But I just could not get used to someone else shaving me. I always did it myself." Lucius rubbed the three-day growth on his chin. "It's hard enough staying clean shaven in this permanent camp. It will be impossible to do it in the field. That's why I am willing to go through this treatment."

Bolanus placed the terracotta cup near the fire to heat the sticky mixture as he said, "I have been talking with the German cavalry auxiliaries. They know what it is like to live in the cold and they say having a thick beard in the winter does not really keep you warmer. Any moisture, including your own snot and spit, will get frozen and stuck in your beard and will make you colder. They also said we should have more than tunics to wear in the cold. Some of the veterans have adopted wearing trousers or wrapping their legs with strips of cloth when they are in the cold north."

When the pot's contents bubbled a little, Bolanus said, "Get ready, Lucius!"

He used a twig with frayed ends to brush a thick molten liquid on Lucius's cheeks and chin. Before it solidified, he covered the fluid with a cloth, which soaked into the now tacky substance. The others smiled as they watched, ready with anticipation to heckle him and laugh at Lucius's discomfort. But Lucius barely winced as the resin was brushed on his cheeks and chin.

"Anybody else?"

Philippus quickly volunteered and was pasted up as well. Bolanus let his friend do the honor, since he was practiced in the method. He peeled back the edge of the cloth just behind Lucius's jaws, one hand on each side. Without any warning, he jerked both hands back. Lucius expelled curse words that even his friends had not heard before. But then, he smiled, red-faced and trying to hide the pain.

"It's not so bad!" The process was repeated with a small strip above his lips. His reaction was more subdued.

The others could not resist joining in as one by one they submitted to the painful procedure. Each time, their friends hooted and hollered, thrilled to watch each other, and attracting other legionaries. Their centurion investigated to make sure the ruckus was indeed harmless.

Marius was still stern, "Men, have your fun. When we are in enemy territory this kind of behavior will not be tolerated."

A courier arrived to distribute mail. Mediolanum was the farthest point north where mail was delivered other than by special military courier. Lucius's name was called and as he opened the letter he saw the Tullii family signet on the wax seal. He was surprised that the letter was from Tullia and not Cicero.

Dear Brother,

Our family has been wracked with one tragedy after another. My father, as you know, had been proclaimed a savior of Rome, honored for exposing Catilina's conspiracy and was much loved by the people. When his consulship ended, however, patricians still loyal to Catilina were elected.

The Republic is in danger. Caesar, Pompey, and Crassus have taken control of the government by forming a triumvirate. The Senate approved of their shared dictatorship. Father was asked to join their cause but he refused to participate. Realizing the danger in this decision, Father has voluntarily chosen exile in Athens.

My husband Piso passed away. He was very kind to me and proved to be an honest man. Supportive of my father's opinions, Piso had addressed the Senate several times. However, he did not convince them to pardon my father and recall him from exile. He then waited for days outside the Senate building in all weather, trying to influence Senators. He caught a terrible fever, and no treatment helped. I have moved back into my mother's house. I am praying that you will safely return to us.

Love, Tullia

Lucius read the letter several times, each time becoming

more anxious. An almost uncontrollable urge made Lucius want to flee to Rome and help his adopted family. He ached to be with Tullia. After calming down, he realized the only way to help was to write to Tullia. As he composed the letter, he thought of telling her he loved her and wanted to be with her, but he knew this was not the time. Instead he encouraged her to take heart and reminded Tullia that her father was a brilliant man and would soon return to Rome with a great plan. He ended his letter with a promise to write frequently because he assumed his legion would winter in Mediolanum and continue to train there until the spring. Then they would probably relieve the garrisoned legions in Gaul.

The next morning after their meal, as the legionaries prepared for training, they were diverted by the sound of bugles and instead assembled with their own units for orders. Marius addressed the 80 men he commanded in his century, including Lucius's squad.

"The Gallic tribes north of the Alps have revolted. One legion has been destroyed and Roman colonists have been massacred. All the legions at Mediolanum will immediately break camp and march to our comrades' relief.

"Legionaries, ready your armor, weapons, and packs. Decurions, supervise the loading of cooking gear, tents and food supplies on your mules. I will return within the hour to organize our place in the marching formations in the cohort. Pack only three days of rations. The tribunes will determine which food and provisions will be transported by the supply train which will follow. In these conditions, we will only be able to bring the light artillery, the scorpions, and we may be asked to carry them on our mules. Men, get ready to cross the Alps."

After Marius boomed his orders to the men he pounded his

right fist into his chest and shouted, "Virtus!"

There was a hesitation among the men and he waited as the sound of their unsynchronized salutes ended. He bellowed even louder, "Virtus!"

This time, the legionaries answered as one with a roaring, "Virtus!"

On the second day north from Mediolanum, the trail became steeper. Throughout the march, Caesar paced up and down the lines and joined the centurions as they encouraged the men to maintain their pace. Caesar shouted, "Fellow soldiers, our comrades are outnumbered in Gaul and are awaiting your help. Two hundred years ago, Hannibal used this same pass and crossed the Alps in fifteen days. Can you beat that? Are you going to let Carthaginians outmarch you? Outmarch a Roman legionary? Never! Comrades march!"

#

Several days later, they arrived at the summit of a high mountain pass, the trail covered in snow. As the legions started downhill, Lucius could barely remember how they had gotten there. His memory was a blur: placing one foot in front of the other, having short sleeps, walking through the night, waiting to start marching again.

They reached Transalpine Gaul and made camp. Caesar sent out scouts to locate the enemy. Meanwhile, remnants of the Roman legions that had been defeated by the Gauls filtered into the camp. Their accounts spread quickly through the ranks. Lucius reported to his tent what he had heard.

"Caesar has completely surprised the Gauls with his speed. Vercingetorix assumed we could not come before the spring. The

Gauls are scattered and occupied attacking those towns still allied with Rome. For the first time, however, almost all the Gallic tribes are united for one cause, led by Vercingetorix."

Philippus added, "I heard after he defeated a Roman legion, he gained the fanatic loyalty of all the Gauls. They are not taking any prisoners. They have massacred all the Roman merchants and citizens in the towns they have taken."

Lucius looked around at the men.

"Vercingetorix may be a charismatic leader and a good strategist, but remember we have Caesar leading us. Get your sleep. Caesar does not want to lose his advantage of surprise. We march tomorrow morning."

Caesar's legions quickly captured three Gallic towns. Vercingetorix, however, refused to oppose Caesar in open battle. Instead he destroyed grain supplies and bridges, and he burned towns to hinder Caesar's progress. The Romans finally caught up with Vercingetorix at the city of Gergovia. Vercingetorix had the advantage. The town was situated on a plateau fifteen hundred feet above the surrounding plain and had almost impregnable defenses. Caesar's plan was to draw them out, since the Romans were short on supplies and a long, protracted siege of the city was not feasible.

Rather than boxing his forces inside the walled city, Vercingetorix strategically kept his forces mobile and occupied the high ground around Gergovia. Caesar countered by sending a legion to dislodge elements of these outlying Gallic forces north of the city. When Vercingetorix took the bait, and sent troops to recapture the hill, Caesar sent three legions, including the Sixth Legion, to scale the walls of Gergovia. They were to engage the enemy on the walls, and then feign retreat. If successful, they would draw the enemy down to the plain in front of the city. The

Tenth Legion waited there in reserve.

The Sixth Legion marched up the slope in maniple formation. As they drew closer to the walls, spears, arrows, and rocks rained down on them. The centurions signaled for each century to organize into a testudo. Each of these groups, comprised of 80 men, formed a densely-packed rectangle which indeed, resembled a turtle. The inside men held their rectangular shields above their heads to protect against missiles and the outside men used their shields to protect the perimeters of the formation.

Marius Duilius took command of his testudo formation as he shouted, "Ready! Testudo! Move! Left foot—step! Right foot, slide up! Left foot—step! Right foot, slide up." After he initiated the command, the formation moved in unison to the city wall. "Left! Right! Left! Right!"

The clatter of spears, rocks and debris plummeting them was thunderous but then it quieted a little. Lucius looked up and noticed some of the defenders on the wall were directing their attention elsewhere.

"Scale the wall!" Marius shouted.

Grappling hooks with ropes were thrown and ladders hoisted. Lucius noticed several men climbed to the top without opposition. However, when he ascended the wall, the fighting was furious and took the form of man-to-man combat. Lucius knew the Roman legionaries were skilled fighters, but their strength was not in single combat. Now the larger Gallic warriors had the advantage with their long swords against the shorter Roman stabbing swords. Also, many Romans were without their shields, having dropped them as they had scaled the wall.

Lucius looked about for Marius, hoping an officer would instill some organization to the melee. He did not see him or any other centurion, so he organized his own squad of eight into a compact fighting unit. As more Romans reached the top of the walls, they joined his group to hold the immediate area of the wall allowing more of the legionaries to reach the top.

Against orders, many of the Romans who reached the top of the wall became overconfident and rashly moved into the city. Lucius saw a large detachment of Gallic cavalry flood the streets and town square, engaging the Roman soldiers.

The Roman bugles sounded the retreat, as was planned, but hundreds of legionaries did not heed the signal. Lucius also blew his whistle and shouted for the insubordinate soldiers to withdraw. There were now more than a thousand Romans in the city, flushed with a sense of victory and thoughts of booty.

"Don't you know what the bugle signal means?" shouted a centurion just below Lucius's squad at the base of the wall. "Get your asses down here now!"

Lucius sent his men down the ropes and decided he would be the last to follow. His final glance into the city showed scores of legionaries being cut down. Then, a large contingent of Gallic cavalry made a sortie outside the city and crashed into the legionaries who were retreating from the walls. Three legions were in unorganized flight across the plain as they were pursued by the enemy cavalry.

Below the city on the plain, Caesar watched the retreat with his officers as they stood with the Tenth Legion, which had been held in reserve. The Tenth was the crack legion in the army. The legionaries of the Tenth had the most experience, were the most professional soldiers of the Roman army, and were intensely loyal to Caesar. He had trained the legion himself.

"What the hell is going on?" Caesar shouted to his tribunes. "We waited too late to pull back. This was to be an organized retreat. Pavius, move the Tenth forward in quick time. Supply each man with two extra javelins to hit the Gallic cavalry. Set up the maniples to funnel the fleeing legionaries back to the camps, and then flood the gaps with scorpion missiles when the Gauls follow them. How many German cavalry are available?"

"Eight hundred, Caesar," Pavius answered.

"Have them wait in the rear. When the Gauls approach the Tenth, move the Germans to cover the Tenth's flanks and then if conditions allow, continue forward to envelop the enemy."

#

Lucius, still atop the wall, prepared to lower himself down. When he saw several wounded legionaries needing help, he waved his squad below to go ahead. As Lucius helped the wounded down, he was startled by the din of the Gallic cavalry crashing into the advancing Tenth Legion.

Lucius reached the base of the city wall. A legionary wearing the uniform of the standard bearer wandered about in a daze, and seemed to be searching abandoned equipment. He called out something incoherent. Lucius negotiated his way among fallen bodies, rocks, and debris to reach the legionary. At the man's feet was a long pole affixed with the standard of the Sixth Legion, topped by a golden sculpture of an eagle.

"Standard bearer!" Lucius said. "Why would you abandon the Aquila? Soldier, your duty was to stay with the legion. The Aquila is the heart and spirit of the Sixth!"

The legionary raised the Aquila. "I will take it back to the legion." He carried the eagle atop the eight-foot staff, marching as if he were leading the legion into battle. The standard bearer began picking his way through the rocks at the base of walls toward the plain where the battle raged between the Tenth and the Gallic cavalry.

Lucius ran to chase him down and shouted, "Stop! You will walk right into the Gauls and lose the Aquila to the enemy!" Before Lucius could reach him, the man stumbled and fell to the ground, dead from wounds inflicted in the battle.

Lucius was disheartened by the loss of another Roman comrade. But he found consolation as he watched the battle below him on the plain. The veteran Tenth Legion, supported by a barrage of missiles from the scorpions and aided by the German cavalry, broke the Gallic attack. Most of Vercingetorix's warriors returned to Gergovia's fortress, but many remained on the battlefield looking for loot and trophies. Lucius watched the Roman troops retreat to their fortified camps and wondered if his squad had returned alive. His path to join them was blocked by the enemy.

That night, Lucius dared not cross the plain to the Roman camps. He found a small ravine and hid among underbrush and trees. Enemy soldiers were moving about, looting the dead and finishing off the Roman wounded. He was fortunate that they were rogue warriors and not an organized search, or he might have been discovered.

#

The next morning the Romans exited their camps and Caesar tried again to lure Vercingetorix out of the city to fight on the plain. The legions formed their ranks as Caesar discussed the situation with his staff. The group ranged from veteran centurions, who had worked their way through the ranks, to new tribunes, young patricians with little military experience.

"We lost almost a thousand men yesterday, including fifty centurions. Most of the losses were from the Sixth Legion, who were the first to scale the walls. This morning, it was reported the Sixth's Aquila is missing," Pavius reported.

"That is a bad omen." Caesar commented and then paused. "The Sixth is a new legion without much experience, but experience is the teacher of all things and they will be stronger.

"Vercingetorix has learned much over the last few years. He has destroyed food and supplies ahead of our advances and even burned his own towns. This resulting lack of supplies will change our strategy. Several years ago, they would have stayed in their walled cities, and we would have starved them out or breached their walls. Now they are denying us provisions. Vercingetorix is a good tactician and will not fight unless he has an advantageous position. If he holds out, we will run out of food. Instead, we'll go north to join Titus Labienus, with his four legions and adequate supplies."

Then they felt a low pulsation from the ground as the assembled legionaries jostled and shuffled, followed by unintelligible hum and chatter. Caesar was distressed that his disciplined soldiers were displaying such unrestrained behavior. The murmurs rose into scattered shouts and then built into a roar from thousands of legionaries. Added to the clamor was loud crashing as the soldiers beat their swords on their shields. The legionaries of the Sixth Legion, although battered and wounded, bellowed the loudest of all.

Marching across the open ground toward the assembled mass was Lucius, his uniform shredded and tattered. He proudly held the Sixth's standard high above his head, the gold eagle flashing in the sun. Twenty-five thousand Romans shouted,

"AQUILA! AQUILA! AQUILA!"

4 ALESIA

As the legions moved through central Gaul, the Gallic revolt continued into the summer. Lucius endured the heat marching with his heavy pack. It had been two months since the battle at Gergovia. Caesar had joined his legions with his second in command, Legate Titus Labienus, who had four additional legions. Now with more food and supplies obtained in the north, the combined forces had successfully besieged several cities. Vercingetorix followed the Romans and frequently skirmished with their rearguard but refused to commit to full battle. As Lucius kept a steady pace with his comrades, he recounted his relief when he had discovered his entire squad had survived the battle at Gergovia. However, a pall had hung over the men of his century for weeks, as they mourned the death of their centurion Marius.

Lucius could see the legions stretched out ahead of him as they marched down a long hill into an open country of meadows. The combined forces of the Roman army now included forty thousand infantry. Six of the legions were marching ahead of the

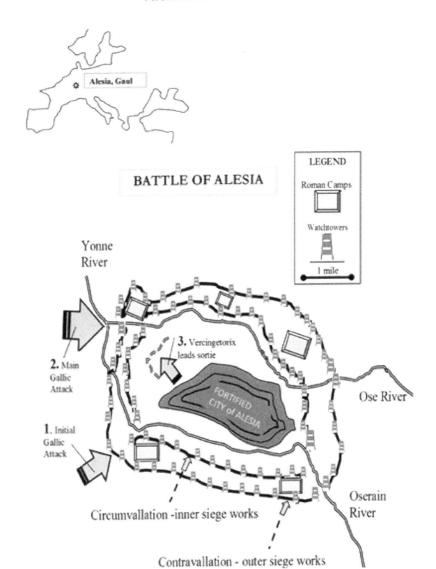

BATTLE OF ALESIA

Alesia, Gaul

LEGEND

Roman Camps

Watchtowers

1 mile

Yonne River

3. Vercingetorix leads sortie

2. Main Gallic Attack

FORTIFIED CITY of ALESIA

Ose River

1. Initial Gallic Attack

Oserain River

Circumvallation -inner siege works

Contravallation - outer siege works

baggage train. The Sixth and the Tenth legions formed the rearguard marching behind the baggage. Several thousand Roman and German cavalry flanked the marching columns. Lucius knew from his experience at Gergovia that Vercingetorix's Gallic cavalry alone numbered upwards of twenty thousand. To counter, Caesar had enlisted thousands of mounted German troops to bolster the small number of Roman cavalry. But when Caesar had found that the horses of the German cavalry were weak from malnourishment, he had ordered replacements from the Roman cavalry.

Lucius heard shouts and discovered a skirmish developing between the Tenth Legion rearguard and the Gallic cavalry. He immediately called to the other decurions to organize the men into maniples. Instead of another skirmishing party, however, the enemy force was comprised of thousands of mounted warriors.

Pavius redirected the Sixth to form lines three deep to prevent the Gauls from outflanking them. The first cavalry charge was repelled by a hail of javelins. Caesar arrived and ordered the infantry to form a rectangle to surround their baggage train and protect the foodstuffs.

While the infantry repelled the attacks, the chief cavalry officer, Antonius Marcus, had organized the Roman cavalry, combined forces with the Germans, and staged a counterattack. Lucius and his fellow legionaries roared their encouragement as Marcus chased the Gallic army from the battlefield.

Within several hours, the infantry arrived within sight of the hilltop fortress-city of Alesia, where the Gallic army had fled. Lucius surveyed the city. *These fortifications will be more difficult to scale than Gergovia. The city is on a plateau between two rivers and it towers above the surrounding valley. The Gauls are driving cattle into their stronghold, preparing for a siege.*

Shortly after the Gallic troops entered Alesia, the legions began construction of their fortified camps. Before nightfall, the Sixth had completed their camp. Lucius's squad was resting around their campfire recovering from an afternoon of heavy labor, digging trenches and constructing palisades. Lucius sipped vinegar wine.

"Well, men, it looks like Caesar will not let us be bored. I was just told that tomorrow we will begin a circumvallation of Alesia."

None of his tent mates commented. Then Philippus said, "Professor Bolanus, please tell us, what is a circum, uh, a circumvallation?"

"Hmmm. Let's see. Yes, yes, in my extensive studies, I read that is one of the ancient rites of the wood nymphs who live in this region. First, we must make love to the lovely nymphs. If the fairies are pleased, they will dance around the valley naked until Alesia's walls fall down."

A chorus of laughs and groans halted when Lucius interjected, "To form a circumvallation of Alesia, we will build fortifications and walls that will surround the city. The Gauls will be our prisoners."

Before anyone could comment, a tall tribune with an aquiline nose, unknown to those in Lucius's squad, approached them and saluted. Lucius stood up and returned the salute.

Without any introduction, the tribune spoke. "I'll need a short sword and shield. My long cavalry sword, good from atop of my horse, will be no use in the infantry." He removed his helmet and his dark curly hair sprung out, long for a Roman soldier. "And find me a better helmet. This tribune crest will no longer do."

Lucius was surprised the man did not introduce himself. Formal military etiquette had somewhat fallen by the wayside due to the hardship of long and weary months on the battlefield. Yet, Lucius assumed he was an educated patrician and thought it was an irritating way to introduce himself. But the tribune was a ranking officer, and Lucius responded accordingly.

"Will you be commanding our cohort, sir?"

The stranger did not answer, but kept on his first subject.

"You didn't hear? Caesar gave the Germans most of our horses because their steeds were sick and weak! They took my prize horse brought from the Nebrodi Mountains in Sicily. Now who knows what will happen to her. Those Germans do not know how to treat these kinds of mounts, the best horses in Italy!"

Philippus, not one to listen long to such talk, interjected, "I guess the proconsul decided to give the best horses to the best riders!"

"Watch out, soldier, I will be your centurion soon!" The newcomer snapped.

The rest of the squad, too tired to care about this irksome boor, remained quiet, hoping he would soon depart. They had been insulated from nobles like him, military tribunes who were usually on staff with the Legate or Caesar. Then suddenly they were alert, as several of them looked wide-eyed behind the tribune. They jumped to their feet. The tribune turned to see Caesar striding toward them with the Sixth's commander, Quintus Tullius Cicero, and the centurion Pavius rushing to keep pace. Caesar was carrying a centurion's helmet.

The tribune smiled, and as he turned and saw the

approaching men, he announced to the squad, "And it looks like I will be commissioned by the proconsul himself!"

Caesar addressed the tribune. "Not quite, Tribune Gnaeus, or should I say Legionary Gnaeus. That type of behavior is why you are being demoted. You have not contributed to my staff with any creative strategy. My man, don't you know, creating is the essence of life! You do not have the experience a tribune needs to lead a cohort. The German horse traded for your Sicilian mount is dead, so you cannot continue in the cavalry. Where are your skills? You must work your way from basics upward and prove yourself, and then we shall see. This squad is made up of fine soldiers. Work with them and you will find the way. Your ambition and ego will carry you far if you channel them right, but you need experience and the proper tools to get there. I promised your father, Calvinus, that you'd return a soldier, and you will. You'll thank me later."

Caesar turned to face Lucius and held out the helmet. The helmet was well polished and fitted with a red crest made of stiff horse-hair. The crest was attached transversely across the helmet. This afforded the legionaries the ability to easily find and follow their centurion's movements during battle. Caesar held the helmet out toward Lucius.

"No, Gnaeus," he continued, "this helmet is for Aquila."

"Sir?" Lucius stood astounded with his arms hanging loosely at his sides.

"At Gergovia, we realized we had to retreat, so our morale was very low. But when the men saw you marching across the field with immense pride, bearing the Sixth's Aquila, we left the battlefield feeling united and stronger. Slight forces of fortune can have a great deal of power in war and can bring about great changes. The men of the Sixth have given you a new name. You have earned it, Aquila—Lucius Pontius Aquila." Caesar nodded at Philippus and said, "Philippus, you will replace Aquila as decurion."

Caesar saluted, pounding his fist to his chest.

"Virtus, comrades in arms!"

The men all responded in unison, "Virtus!"

Caesar turned on his heel and briskly departed, accompanied by Quintus.

Pavius, seeing Philippus was surprised and stunned, added, "Philippus, if you take care of your men as well as Lucius, uh, as well as Aquila did," he said with a smile, "you will all survive to become prosperous from this campaign. Caesar generously rewards men of skill and action. Aquila, you are going to have a busy evening. Meet me at the headquarters within the hour. We need to inform the rest of the century of your promotion. Caesar's preeminent general, Titus Labienus, wants to meet you."

As Pavius departed, the squad sat back down to prepare their evening meal.

"Whew! What just happened?" Philippus blurted out with an exhalation of air. "How did Caesar know my name?"

Ricimer, not impressed, replied, "I am sure Pavius told him."

"No, Caesar knows just about everybody's name in all the legions," Bolanus added.

"You idiot, that's impossible," Ricimer answered. He and

his comrades looked up at Gnaeus, still standing, now officially part of the squad, but looking disassociated from all of them, especially after his crude start. "You were on Caesar's staff. What about Caesar knowing everybody's name in the legions?"

"It is closer to the truth than you think. Caesar pays attention to every detail and seems to be everywhere all the time. He is full of energy and ideas, constantly soliciting his staff's opinion on them. He never seems to sleep. At night when most of us are asleep, he is writing and recording the events of the war. Haven't you noticed him checking and working on the camp's fortifications during the last months? He will slip in and be gone before you knew he was there. He has probably worked beside you and you did not even know it. He doesn't just know our names, but he treats us as fellow soldiers, as comrades."

"How did that come out of your mouth, fellow, when Caesar himself just struck you down with his tongue?" asked Ricimer.

"I say this out of respect, not affection."

Despite Gnaeus's initial attitude, Lucius was interested in hearing what Gnaeus had to say, but duty called and he left to meet the senior officers.

#

The men were preparing to turn in for the night when Lucius returned. He sat down next to the fire. They laughed as they shared bread and drank vinegar wine with Gnaeus.

Philippus said to Lucius, "So, Centurion Lucius Pontius Aquila, do we now have to call you sir? You left so fast we were not able to congratulate you on your promotion. Today Centurion, tomorrow Primus Pilus!"

Lucius rolled his eyes. Ricimer chuckled as he said, "You mean the longest javelin!"

The conversation continued to degrade into perversion as the legionaries hooted and howled. One of them snorted and said between laughs, "The longest, the biggest. He shouldn't be called Primus Pilus but Primus Phallus; the biggest phallus in the legion!"

As Lucius lay down to sleep, he recalled the meeting earlier in the evening with Titus Labienus, Caesar's second in command. *His style of leadership does not match the charisma of Caesar, but the legate has demonstrated brilliance in battle that matches his superior's. Titus is from an equestrian family and is a strong supporter of the Republic. He was elected to Tribune of the Plebeians a decade ago, and supported Caesar politically in many of his ventures. They have become close friends. He said he was more comfortable in his military career than the political one he left. That is interesting. I am following the opposite path, establishing myself in the military, then politics later.*

The next morning, Lucius's first experience leading his century was not in battle but in digging ditches and constructing the palisades to surround and trap the enemy in Alesia. As his ten squad leaders sat in a semi-circle outside his tent, Aquila used his centurion's staff to trace a map of the area around Alesia.

"These are the plans I learned last night at the centurions' staff meeting, Lucius said. "Wooden palisades will be constructed fifteen feet high around Alesia. The circumvallation will need to be about ten miles long to surround the Gallic fortress. Wooden towers, equipped with ballistae and catapults, will be built into the palisade at these marked intervals. To hinder the enemy's approach to the palisade, two ditches will be constructed, here and here. We will flood one of the ditches by diverting water from the river. A series of holes will be dug in front of the ditches and filled with sharpened sticks, iron hooks, and other traps."

Philippus said, "We are used to constructing the fortified camps, but these tasks are new."

Lucius answered, "Our century's first work will be ditch digging, which you all know and love. Engineers from each legion's First Cohort will arrive today to guide and train us in the palisade construction."

A second squad leader added, "I know my men will not complain about the hard work, since the alternative would be attacking the high ground and then the walls of Alesia. I assume we will be out of armor when working. Will we also alternate on guard duty?"

"Because of the need for mobility, the Roman cavalry, aided by the German auxiliaries, will be on standby and repel any Gallic cavalry sorties if they attempt to hinder our work. The infantry will be assigned to work on the fortifications."

#

During the second week of construction, before the circumvallation was completed, a group of the Gallic cavalry escaped. Expecting that a relief force would now be sent, Caesar ordered a second line of fortifications to be built, a contravallation, facing outward and enclosing the legions between it and the first set of walls. Within three weeks, the inner fortifications were completed. Construction then began on the outer line, identical to the first in design. The contravallation extended for over eighteen miles in circumference. The outer wall was completed and the legionaries performed daily drills to practice maneuvering among the fortifications.

#

After several weeks of drills, one morning Lucius heard the bugle sound and exited his tent. He noted there were no enemy activities across the river at Alesia and assumed it announced the start of another one of the frequent drills they had been conducting since the fortifications had been completed. Men groaned and whined as Philippus and his squad stumbled out of a nearby tent.

"Another drill!"

"Look up men; at least we are not digging ditches any longer," Philippus responded.

"There are not enough troops to man all the palisades. We must be able to rapidly move reinforcements around the siege works. You will appreciate that Caesar is pushing us so hard, when the training ultimately saves our lives," Lucius added.

After the drill, Caesar decided the men were ready and announced that the legionaries would be free to have some recreation. The merchants who followed the legions were also encamped within the fortifications. Visits to the camp followers, traders, and merchant tents for female companionship were strictly limited and controlled by permission from the officers. In their free time, most legionaries resorted to playing dice or bocce combined with betting and gambling. The vinegar supply was still intact, and drafts of the sour wine were a popular currency for betting.

#

A few weeks after Caesar had relaxed the training schedule,

Aquila was making his rounds. Philippus sat outside his tent with his squad chipping away at stones with their pickaxes. Their labors had produced a pile of spherical stones about four inches in diameter.

Aquila said, "Philippus, you are a real craftsman. Are you going to make that stone perfectly round?"

"Yes. The more round the ammunition, the more accurate the scorpions will shoot." He kissed another completed stone and threw it on the pile and said, "When we run out of bolts for the scorpions, these stones will crush a few barbarian skulls. But we will use the perfect stones for our bocce game. And let me show you what I have devised."

As they approached a rectangle formed on the ground by logs five or six inches in diameter, Lucius said. "It looks about the size of a bocce area. So, you will play within the logs instead of just scratching lines in the dirt?"

"Of course. It is four paces wide and twenty-five paces long. The game will be even more interesting as the stones can also be deflected off the logs."

Over the next few days, Philippus won many of the matches with his carefully formed stones. His newly designed court increased the participants' enthusiasm. Philippus's mates became frustrated with his continued successes. Finally, one day, as Philippus collected his winnings from yet another match, Gnaeus threw his hands up in the air, admitting complete defeat, and shouted, "All right, I give up. You are my uncle, my best uncle!"

#

Several days later, Aquila climbed one of the watchtowers

and surveyed the placement of the legions, camps, and fortifications. His enjoyment of the fine, sunny day with cool breezes was interrupted by the hunger pangs in his stomach. The legionaries had been on reduced rations approaching a month. He then heard the high-pitched voices of women and children coming from within the walls of Alesia.

The front gates of the Alesian stronghold opened and hundreds of women and children filed out. Aquila was astonished. The Gallic forces were running out of food and they had decided to sacrifice women and children to preserve rations for the fighting men. All day the unfortunate could be heard wailing as they traveled back and forth between Alesia's walls and the Roman fortifications, pleading for food or to be let through to the outside. They settled that night at the base of the walls of Alesia, subject to starvation and exposure.

On September 1, the fifty-eighth day of the siege, the quietude of the morning was broken by shouts and commotion from the enemy sentries manning the walls of Alesia, and from the Roman watchtowers as well. On a broad grassy hill to the northwest of the valley, a huge formation of Gallic warriors had appeared. The valley rolled with the sound of tens of thousands of warriors' shouts, cheers, and battle cries, answered by their brethren in Alesia. The evening and night were filled with the reverberations of the huge army setting their camps.

#

The following morning, Aquila sat in a circle in front of Pavius's tent with the other nine centurions of the Sixth Legion. Pavius had just returned from Caesar's staff meeting and was disseminating the strategy. Sounds of troops marching and horses galloping echoed in the hills around them, announcing the arrival of more Gallic reinforcements. Pavius drew a map in the dirt showing the location of the Roman and Gallic forces and fortifications. He pointed with his centurion's rod at two points, one at the northwest corner and the other at the southwest corner of the circumvallation.

"Here and here . . . the rivers cut through palisades and make these points subject to breaching. Caesar believes this is where they will try to break through. It is no secret how many warriors they have. They have camped on that hill in plain view to unnerve us with their numbers. Aquila, how many Gallic reinforcements have arrived?"

"The sentries reported just over two hundred thousand in the last few days, sir."

"Comments, Aquila?"

"Sir, the enemy inside Alesia can see the movements of the reinforcements outside the circumvallation and vice versa, so no doubt they will coordinate and attack our weakest points simultaneously from both sides of our fortifications."

"Yes, so we must ensure we march the infantry reserves closely along the inside of the walls to screen their movement."

Pavius addressed the centurion sitting next to Aquila.

"Lentilus, did you complete the obstructions in front of Alesia's gate?"

"Yes, sir, the only route the Gallic troops can use to exit Alesia is blocked by a deep ditch. The vertical sides will prevent their horses from crossing. The field has been strewn with sharpened sticks and mantraps. The route is within range of the scorpions on the watchtowers."

"Good, but Vercingetorix is exceptionally clever, and we

should expect that the obstacles will slow him but not stop him."

Pavius scanned the circle and made sure he locked onto each centurion's eyes.

"There are not enough legionaries to man all the palisades, which makes it that much more important that we communicate well, move fast, and be flexible enough to meet these threats. The Sixth will be asked to move into these vulnerable areas as reinforcements. We believe the assault will happen very soon."

As Pavius stood, the centurions also came to their feet.

"Trust your training, trust each other and we will win."

He saluted as they all called out, "Virtus!"

Aquila returned to his century and briefed his men. He assembled them near a watchtower and palisade, currently patrolled by other legionaries.

When he announced the battle was imminent, a legionary confidently shouted, "Good, the sooner the better. Let's fight. I'm tired of waiting!" His proclamation was followed by a chorus of statements in agreement. *Good! Despite all the tiresome days, they still have the zeal to fight.*

Within hours bugles sounded for the Romans to man their defensive posts. The huge Gallic camp came alive and the mass of warriors split into two large columns. One contingent advanced down the hill toward the southwest corner of the outer siegeworks. The larger body of troops turned north and disappeared around the back of a hill. The gate of Alesia opened and infantry carrying bales of hay exited, followed by a large force of cavalry.

Quintus Tullius Cicero, the Legate of the Sixth Legion, and

Pavius rushed among the legionaries encouraging them as they prepared for the battle. As the two officers arrived at Aquila's century, a messenger dismounted, and reported to Quintus.

"Sir, Caesar affirms that the attack forming near the southwest corner between Camps Four and Five will not be the enemy's primary thrust. Instead, the larger contingent that disappeared behind the hill will assault the northwest wall at the breaks in the river. Caesar orders two cohorts of the Sixth to be sent as reserves to the expected location of attack before the enemy arrives."

Quintus addressed Aquila, "I am sending the Second Cohort to stand in reserve of the Tenth Legion at the river. Lead your century at fast pace ahead of them and notify Legate Labienus as soon as you are in position. Pavius will follow with the First Cohort."

Aquila looked across the river as he rushed with his men down to the northwest wall. Outside the citadel of Alesia, the enemy infantry began throwing hay into the ditches that blocked the road from the city to the river. Vercingetorix led a large force of cavalry out of the gate and waited as the infantry continued to fill the deep ditch with hay. *Our long hours of labor constructing the ditch have paid off. The Alesian cavalry is stalled and the legionaries defending at the southwest will not have to fight on two battlefronts.*

In the distance, across the river and beyond Alesia, Lucius could see the enemy assaulting the southwest fortifications. The enemy was well prepared and had brought battering rams, hooks, ropes, ladders, and torches. Even though the Gauls were still over one hundred paces away, the Roman defenders fired large iron arrows into their ranks from the scorpions located in the watchtowers. The arrows punched gaping holes in the mass of men.

When the enemy approached within twenty paces of the palisades, the legionaries' javelins were thrown en masse. A second wave of javelins and a third were thrown, which thinned the front ranks. Large numbers of Gallic warriors replaced the fallen, and the assault continued to roll toward the walls.

As each charge failed to breach the walls, the Gauls would retreat, but another fresh group of attackers would emerge from the mass and throw themselves against the defenders. The Roman defense weakened, and the Gauls broke through a small section of the outer wall. Roman infantry formed two lines of three deep in time to prevent the enemy from breaching the hole.

A signal was sent to the cavalry camp for help. The Gallic axes and swords crashed down onto the Roman infantry, but were unable to break through their wall of rectangular shields.

The legionaries took a huge toll on the Gallic warriors, stabbing with their short swords under the arcs made by the Gallic long swords and axes.

The surge from the mass of Gallic foot soldiers compressed the Roman front lines, and they could not fall back to be relieved by the second and third lines. The exhausted front line collapsed and most were slain.

The commanding centurion timed his next maneuver to coordinate with the cavalry reinforcements coming from the south. Just as they arrived, he blew a signal on his high-pitched bone whistle. Roman infantry lines wheeled with one end of the line anchored at the wall. The Gauls pushed through the void and were caught between the two Roman units. Piles of Gallic dead impeded additional Gallic incursions, and the Roman lines were reformed to block the opening in the wall.

The Gallic cavalry from Alesia was still not able to advance. However, a group of their accompanying infantry had scrambled across the ditch. Their Gallic brethren outside the wall renewed their onslaught at the breach when they saw their success.

Lucius and his men waited at the river in reserve next to a cavalry detachment. A courier ran up out of breath and shouted he needed a horse to take a message from Caesar to the southwest battlefront. As a horse was led to him he shouted, "They asked Caesar for more reinforcements at the southwest battle. His officers recommended another cavalry unit be sent, but Caesar answered he will not commit reserves until he discovers the intent of the other Gallic column behind the hill. Instead, I am to tell the legionaries at the southwest breach to defend and hold their position."

As the courier galloped off, the larger Gallic relief column appeared from behind the hill, marching in the shallows of the river. They charged through a discontinuity in the fortifications, where the palisade could not be erected in the river, initiating a second battlefront. Roman infantry maniples from the Tenth Legion blocked the assault and the fighting was furious. Legionaries from the Sixth, including Aquila's unit, stood on the flanks in reserve, hidden by the palisades. There was very little room to maneuver and the Tenth's maniples could not wheel and reinforce each other in the traditional method.

Labienus gave instructions to his tribunes to create a pincer formation. As the Gallic warriors charged up the river through the breach in the wall, the Roman Centurions signaled the Roman maniples to retreat in good order. As the Gauls pushed ahead, those maniples hidden by the palisade struck the Gauls from both sides.

Back at the first battlefront, the southwest corner of the contravallation, the fatigued legionaries faltered after hours of fighting. With the situation getting dangerous for the Romans, Caesar notified his renowned cavalry commander, Antonius Marcus, to deploy reinforcements at his own discretion. Marcus led two cohorts to the breach in the river. Caesar kept twelve cohorts of combined Roman and German cavalry in reserve.

Aquila was encouraged by the arrival of Marcus with the cavalry reinforcements. He checked his century squad leaders and saw that Philippus in his new leadership role was doing well. Looking among the constant rain of spears and arrows that glanced off shields and careened off legionaries' helmets and armor, Aquila tried to stay focused on his men's cohesion and not get distracted by individual combat.

A thousand times if the long Gallic swords had battered the legionaries' shields down a sliver farther, a host of Romans would have taken their last breath. Ten thousand times, spears flashed to implant a crippling blow but were parried by the legionaries. The long hours of training gave the Romans the stamina and skill to sustain the intense fighting. Aquila was exhausted, but each time he repelled an opponent or warded off death another instant, the success fueled his determination even more. There was no time for fear.

During the fighting, Aquila led his men with pride as they held back the Gauls. The Gallic warriors were large, fearsome, and tough fighters. The legionaries were steadfast and united in their defense, but their stamina was faltering as weeks of low rations had taken its toll. The legionaries in formation continued to survive. The ones that stumbled on the maneuvers or were pulled out of line were usually lost. Aquila knew he could not allow the sight of slain comrades to distract him. His disciplined leadership would save more lives than breaking formation to save individuals. He concentrated on keeping the legionaries unified and ensuring they fought as they had been trained. The success of the battle and their lives depended on Aquila making the right decision for the formation in the right instant. The fighting was so sharp that split-second timing was needed to ensure survival. An errant clod of dust in his throat or a missile striking his helmet could interrupt his centurion's whistle, delay a maneuver, and bring on disaster.

The legionaries were fighting as they had been taught, keeping their shields locked together. They ducked and thrust their swords, but they did not lose sight of the enemy. When the legionaries became squeezed against the enemy frontline, they slashed their opponents' legs.

Suddenly, the din of battle increased. The Gallic infantry pulled back and a large group of Gallic cavalry charged through. The change was so sudden that the legionaries did not have time to launch their javelins, their most effective strategy in breaking a cavalry charge. Half the maniple in front of them was trampled. Philippus's maniple reformed at right angles to the Gallic cavalry charge and took out many of them with their javelins. Antonius Marcus led his cavalry to chase down the Gallic cavalry that got through, as the other maniples closed in behind to fill the opening. The Gallic infantry tried to follow and the hand-to-hand slaughter continued. The Gauls repeated this several more times but the Roman response prevented their lines from breaking.

Brutal fighting continued near the river breach as the mass of men and horses churned the ground into a mess of blood, fallen bodies, and slick mud. Aquila saw that Gnaeus was repeatedly losing his footing and falling out of formation. Philippus, the squad's new decurion, moved Gnaeus from the vulnerable right flank and took his place on the right wing of their maniple. The uneven ground challenged even the very agile Philippus.

Rotating with maniples from the Tenth, Aquila pulled back his century from the fighting to rest and drink. He spotted Caesar rushing up and down the lines, bellowing encouragement to the legionaries of the Sixth and Tenth. Caesar then galloped off to the other battlefronts and continued to place himself in dangerous situations on the battlefield. On his next pass by the Tenth, Caesar was convinced by his close friend, cavalry officer Antonius Marcus, and his second in command, Titus Labienus, to retreat and appraise the battle from the vantage point of a watchtower.

The staff officers now with Caesar in the watchtower were several younger and less experienced tribunes whose primary duties were to relay messages out to the legates on the battlefield. As if in a training session, remote from the furious battle, Caesar calmly quizzed one of the tribunes.

"Sevius, describe the situation on the battlefield."

"Sir, the enemy from the Alesian stronghold are about to completely fill the ditch. If they are successful and then breach the undefended inner wall, their cavalry will attack the Tenth and the Sixth from behind, and we will lose. Our defense at the southwest battlement is in danger of collapsing. If the enemy breaks through there, we will lose. We are out of reserves, except for the cavalry cohorts here."

"Good evaluation, Tribune. Now, where is the best use of these reserves and when?" asked Caesar. The tribunes all remained silent. Caesar looked from one tribune to another. "No advice?"

Then a tribune volunteered, "Divide the reserve cavalry into three parts among the two breaches in the walls and against the Alesians crossing the ditch."

"That seems the most logical and the most conservative. We may survive for the time, with an uncertain result, but we need something more decisive. Each of you will go independently and take a message directly to Legate Labienus. At least one of you will make it to Labienus," Caesar answered.

Caesar picked up his bright red cloak and draped it across his back. As he clasped the cloak to his armor, he said, "Tribunes, tell Labienus, no matter how tired his men are, no matter what the odds, no matter what the conditions are, when he sees this cloak they are to stop defending and instead push forward against the enemy."

The three tribunes quickly descended the watchtower and vaulted onto their German horses. Caesar led his cavalry cohorts south in the opposite direction.

One of the tribunes said to Sevius, "I can see Caesar's strategy. He is fleeing! We will be slaughtered here on the battlefield, while he is saving his own neck!"

Sevius drew his cavalry sword and hit the tribune with the flat side, issuing a ringing blow on his helmet. "You have no faith in Caesar? You don't even deserve to be an errand boy on his staff." Disgusted, Sevius galloped away toward Labienus.

Sevius was the first to make it to the Legate Labienus. He shouted over the din of the battle, "Sir, Caesar said when you see his red cloak you are to push forward."

Labienus looked confused.

"The men can hardly stand and they can barely keep their shields up. We are dying here. A push forward outside the walls, even if we had the strength to do it, would expose our flanks."

The tribune did not answer the Legate, but snatched an abandoned shield and short sword. He joined the closest maniple preparing to move back to the front lines, where blood was coursing freely just several paces away.

Suddenly, Labienus saw a flash of bright red beyond the Gauls massed in front of the palisades. Some of the legionaries also saw it and began to shout Caesar's name. The red cloak disappeared momentarily as the Roman cavalry crashed into the back of the Gallic masses. When it reappeared, a roar rose from the legions.

Labienus gave the order to move forward. The sound of bugles and whistles filled the air. The legionaries, exhausted as they were, somehow found new energy. The enemy's ranks wavered. Panic gripped the Gallic forces when they realized they were caught between two pressing forces. They ran without any semblance of a coordinated retreat. When the enemy turned their backs and fled, the Roman infantry was too fatigued to pursue. Many legionaries fell to their knees in exhaustion. The German forces led by Caesar were joined by Marcus with the Roman cavalry. They pursued and slaughtered thousands. Vercingetorix, unable to cross the ditch and seeing his allies crushed, led his starving men back into Alesia.

The next morning Aquila stood in formation with his men and watched with the legions as Vercingetorix surrendered to Caesar. Caesar wanted the Gallic leader's capitulation to be public and assembled the surviving Gallic warriors, women, and children. Vercingetorix knelt before Caesar and appealed that the killing be stopped. Although infuriated that over 12,000 Romans had been killed in the battle, Caesar sent orders to cease pursuit of the scattered Gallic forces. He spared the lives of Gallic prisoners, women and children from Alesia, but retained them as slaves. Each legionary was awarded one slave and most took the value in credit from the slave merchants among the camp followers. The assembly ended, as the prisoners were led away. Aquila asked Pavius, "What will happen to Vercingetorix?"

"He will be taken to Rome and held in the Carcer Mamertine, the state prison, until he is paraded through the city at one of Caesar's triumphs. Following that, the Gallic chief will be executed according to tradition," said Pavius.

"Do you think there will be more fighting?" Aquila asked.

"The news of the Gallic defeat will spread rapidly throughout Gaul. I heard that over one hundred thousand Gauls were slain, and that will convince most of the rebellious tribes to put away their arms."

"What is next for the legions?"

"We are the lucky ones. The Sixth and Tenth Legions are going to Narbo with Caesar, the city from which he governs. The other legions will be garrisoned throughout Gaul."

5 NARBO

Lucius was in a state of absolute bliss. After four years in the field, he had forgotten how much he enjoyed the baths. At Alesia, they had access to the river to wash off a hard day's work. He felt fortunate he wasn't with the legions Caesar had stationed throughout Gaul to maintain peace. Lucius's legion, the Sixth, along with the Tenth, had accompanied Caesar to his base of operations in southern Gaul at the Roman colony of Narbo Martius.

He closed his eyes and relaxed, enveloped by the warm waters and steamy air. A scene flashed into his mind of the baths in Rome. *It seems like it has been more than a few years since I joined my group of friends. We had been eight comrades, which by coincidence, was the number of men that shared a tent. Now there are only four of us left. I miss Egnatius, Bolanus, and Glabrio, but the hardest loss was Philippus. Philippus had commanded the squad just one day, but more men would have been lost had it not been for his bravery. At Alesia Philippus sacrificed himself when he took Gnaeus's place in the most dangerous position of the line. Then Gnaeus filled in for Philippus when he fell. That same Gnaeus, now soaking in the bath next to me, started out with such a self-centered attitude.*

"Time's up!" hollered a centurion with the next group of legionaries. The baths were relatively small and could comfortably hold just a few score of bathers. The legion had to limit the amount of time each soldier could stay; the city's inhabitants were already irritated that their baths were so crowded. Lucius and his friends usually took their time exiting the soothing water, but they noticed Caesar was approaching the bath. All the men quickened their departure. Caesar was known to address his men as comrades-in-arms. He acted the role, as he dug ditches, marched with the infantry, and fought beside his men on the battlefield. These close associations also extended to socializing at the baths.

The governor hailed them.

"Aquila, Gnaeus, stay with me." As Caesar slipped into the water and leaned back on the concrete wall next to Aquila, he said, "The Sixth took heavy losses at Alesia, but you were in the midst of the fiercest fighting and did extremely well. Gnaeus, I understand you did an extraordinary job taking the lead of your tent in the middle of the battle by motivating and protecting your men. I also received a report that after the battle, you saved many lives by preventing your exhausted maniple from breaking the ranks to pursue the barbarians. Indeed, it was best that the cavalry finished the task."

"Yes, Proconsul," Gnaeus answered.

"Both of you have shown great leadership under intense pressure and there are many others who also demonstrated their ability to command. I am confident that you are ready to move a step up, and give your men some room to advance and assume more responsibility. When you return to camp, both of you report to Antonius Marcus for your new assignments."

#

Aquila and Gnaeus made the mile trek to the legions' camp north of Narbo. As they entered the front gate, Aquila said, "It looks like you are going to wear the centurion crest."

"And you, Aquila, will your new rank be Primus Pilus?"

Lucius countered, "That can't happen. Pavius will always be the best man for lead centurion until he retires."

As the pair walked into the cavalry commander's tent, they both halted at attention and saluted Antonius Marcus. He remained slouched in a chair, a cup of wine in his hand, not surprising either one of them when he did not return their salute. It was common knowledge that Marcus was very casual off the field and if one met him for the first time away from the legions, one would not suspect he was a military man. In battle, however, he was unsurpassed as a cavalry commander and was a fearless fighter. He laughed and raised his cup as if toasting them.

"Virtus to you, too, uh, ha, ha . . . Tribunes. Your new helmets and swords are over there on the table. However, you must supply your own horses. But then, most gentlemen do that anyway. The Senate refuses to send us any new supplies, equipment, or recruits."

Gnaeus, delighted to be an officer once again, glanced at Aquila and mouthed, "Tribunes!"

Aquila, however, was more focused on Marcus's last statement and looked puzzled.

"Why does the Senate not support Caesar?"

"The Senate has been hotly contesting Caesar's right to wage war in Gaul. They believe and, of course, they are right, that he uses his conquests to further personal political ambitions, but they also accuse Caesar of using the Republic's legions to become rich from the spoils. You know as well as I do that he gives most of the plunder to his men, except what is needed to resupply the troops. Anyway, unlike me, he prefers a stoic life and, yes, he covets power and fame, but aspirations for great wealth do not drive him."

Marcus rose from his chair, picked up two cups of wine from the table and handed them to Aquila and Gnaeus. They admired the polished tribune helmets and long cavalry swords. Marcus raised his cup and toasted:

"Salute, tribunes!"

As Aquila sipped the red wine, he experienced a taste that was evermore sweeter than he remembered. He had become accustomed to the sour vinegar wine of the legions. Marcus noted their reaction.

"I also savor this wine, which is from Massilia. It is sweeter than I am used to, but a pleasant change. I am pleased with all the wines I have tasted here in Narbonese Gaul, or as most simply call it, the Province. I can help you procure your mounts. I have arranged delivery of what should be some fine horses from Sicily. Any day now, the ship should arrive at the port in Massilia. Gnaeus, your father should be able to afford the cost. Aquila, I am not familiar with your family. Are you of the Pontii clan who are wine merchants?"

Aquila knew that his father showed much discretion in distributing wine and wondered how Marcus knew of his family.

"Sir, I have been away from home for several years, but I am surprised my father's business has become so well-known."

"Well-known? Well, I guess Arenus does keep to himself and does not brand his wine with a Pontii seal, but everyone on the south side of Rome has enjoyed wine distributed by the Pontii for generations."

Aquila felt a burning sensation pass from head to toe. *I have failed to keep my promise to Father to seek out other Pontii and I have only sent two letters from Rome describing my education as an advocate. In my last letter, I told him I was joining Caesar's legions in Gaul. As far as my family knows, I could be dead.*

Aquila responded to Marcus's comment, "I am not familiar with Arenus, uh, Pontius Arenus. My family is in Sicily."

Marcus, still smiling, replied, "Then you know that the Sicilian horses are of the best quality. I can arrange for Gnaeus and you to have first choice of the steeds."

"I should be able to pay with my spoils from Alesia. I have credit for one adult male slave."

"I am afraid that may not be en…

Gnaeus, standing behind Aquila, cleared his throat, and pointed to himself. Marcus continued, "Um, no, no, that's a good trade, Aquila."

Later that afternoon, Aquila wrote several letters. Postal service was provided at Narbo since it was the provincial capital and was on the major road between Italy and Spain. The next morning, his letters to Cicero, Tullia, and his father Marianus were on their way south.

Aquila had never had many opportunities to ride horses, but Gnaeus was an adroit horseman and helped Aquila develop his skills. Their newly issued swords, longer than the standard infantry issue, allowed them to reach down to slash at foot soldiers. For calisthenics, they sparred with heavy wooden swords and practiced mounted charges against targets. Drills included vaulting onto a wooden horse to practice mounting their steeds, a required skill because Roman saddles did not have stirrups. Marcus kept his promise and Gnaeus and Aquila were given first choice in the purchase of Sicilian horses.

Soon Aquila was ready for intensive training in tactics and began drills with the cavalry cohorts. These included the traditional Roman tactic which positioned the cavalry on the wings to prevent the infantry from being outflanked. He also studied the practice Caesar had developed, which used the German cavalry to slow the assault of enemy cavalry on the Roman infantry.

On leave, Aquila rode his new horse into town, where he planned to spend some time at the baths. He left his mount at the stables and stopped at the coach station to check for mail. Rewarded with a letter from Tullia, he sat next to a fountain in the forum, unrolled the scroll and read:

Dear Brother,

Lucius, or should I say, Aquila! Thank you so much for the letter. You are probably wondering how I learned of your new name. Father's younger brother, Uncle Quintus, wrote to us and has kept us informed of your exploits and progress, Tribune Aquila.

In my last letter to you, I told you that my poor husband Piso had died. The following year, I married Furius Crassipes. Our marriage went well. I did not love him, but I was happy. But after two years without having any children, Furius divorced me for someone else. For political reasons, Mother has arranged for me to marry into the Cornelii gens next year.

My husband will be Publius Cornelius Dolabella, one of Pompeius's generals. I guess true love is just wishful poetry. I don't care anymore who they want me to marry. Publius will probably be away at war most of the time anyway. Father, however, does not want me to marry Dolabella, as he thinks it will appear we are committed to Pompeius. Almost in contradiction to this, at Pompeius's request, Father has assumed proconsulship in Asia, to put down revolts and stabilize the area. But, of course, he does this not for Pompeius, but for his love of Rome. Fortunately, he will return this year.

Caesar has asked him a second time to join him in his efforts to lead Rome, but my father continues to be a stalwart supporter of the Republic and resists taking sides at this time. I do not know how he will remain neutral after our family marries into the Cornelii. I forwarded the letter you wrote to him. He sends his love and wishes you to know that he is very proud of his 'Sicilian son.' Will I ever see you again?

Love, Tullia

Aquila wandered along the streets near the forum. *I miss her! It feels as if it has been ten years since I left Rome. The memories of our friendship seem so dim.*

The baths were crowded as usual. Aquila saw Gnaeus and two of his old tent comrades, Ricimer and Juventius, and joined them in the bath. Just as he started to relax, a commotion on the other side of the pool caught their attention. Several of the citizens were shouting at some legionaries. Aquila knew if there were any incidents, the military could lose their privileges at the baths. Several centurions near the conflict quickly intervened and a physical confrontation was avoided.

Juventius sniggered. "It looks as if some citizens have not been training hard enough lately. Maybe they should do a little wrestling before their bath."

Ricimer added, "Those loudmouth citizens might give us a little competition, but most of them here wouldn't be any sport at all. When we first started coming here, the locals wrestled each other, but I haven't seen any of them roughing it up lately. And the officers told us not to wrestle any of the townspeople."

They all looked in surprise at Aquila when he said, "Why don't we just build some of our own baths, like the legions had at Mediolanum? We've added a more permanent palisade to the camp. Our training is going well. I would be interested in something new."

"Who built this one? There must someone in charge of maintenance and operation of the hypocaust," asked Juventus.

"There is," voiced a familiar-looking balding fellow standing nearby, holding several towels. "I helped build these baths almost forty years ago. I am now the caretaker and have been managing the baths since that time."

"We have seen you working around these baths ever since we started coming here and, no offense, sir, but we assumed you were a slave."

"I was, many years ago, but over time I earned enough to buy my freedom. You may wonder why I stay and still do this work? Yes, the municipal office pays me a salary, but the operation of the hypocaust and the baths has always fascinated me. Do you want a tour of the real works of the baths, the hypocaust?"

They nodded and the caretaker threw them each a towel and

said, "Dry off and come with me then." The men, wrapped in their towels, followed the caretaker down a stairway. He began, "Let me remind you that when you entered this building you climbed a staircase, so you can tell that the building is built up above the ground level. Now as we descend under the floor and baths, take note of the numerous brick columns that support the tile floor and concrete baths above you."

A dozen male slaves stoked fires blazing inside brick enclosures.

"Instead of burning a large fire underneath the baths, like you would boil water to cook, we use twigs and wood chips to operate these small furnaces. Then to heat the water in the baths more evenly, the hot air and smoke rising from the fires is vented through these terracotta pipes up and along the sides of the bath and out the roof. The bricks and pipes hold the heat well and transfer it to the passing air. Venting the hot air also prevents the smoke from filling up the bathhouse or hypocaust room where we must work. This type of hypocaust heating system is also used to heat the floors of patricians' houses."

"Who could have invented such a marvelous system?" asked Juventius.

"Years ago, the architect of the baths told me that he was trained by the inventor of the hypocaust, a Roman engineer named Sergius Orata." The caretaker chuckled as he continued, "I heard that Orata made his invention pay off. He had a business where he would buy houses and refit them with hypocausts and resell them for a handsome profit."

The men laughed in approval, as Aquila addressed the caretaker.

"Larger baths are needed for the garrison and the people of

Narbo. If I convinced my Legate to supply the labor, would you ask the city to provide the building material? With your experience and knowledge, we would have better baths than Massilia."

Over the next few months, Aquila organized the men of the Sixth and Tenth legions to build new baths next to the municipal Narbo baths. Completed by the end of the summer, these baths could accommodate three hundred bathers, including plebeian and patrician civilians, and soldiers. The original baths were converted to use for women.

#

It was a warm September evening of the year the patrician Servius Sulpicius Rufus and the plebeian Marcus Claudius Marcellus were consuls. The officers of the Tenth Legion and Sixth Legion gathered in Caesar's large tent used for assemblies. The men stood crowded around tables filled with fresh meat, bread, and pitchers of wine, where they ate and socialized. After he was certain the men had been allowed plenty of time to enjoy themselves, Caesar stood on a table and gained their attention with his signature greeting.

"Comrades! Comrades in arms!"

The men halted their conversations, eager to hear what new venture their commander might have in store for them. Feasts such as these usually accompanied an announcement of a new development or campaign.

"Comrades, as you know, the majority of the senate consists of patricians. They have tried to block my every move to help the people. By bringing Gaul into the realm of Rome, I thought they would see the value of the province. But some of the senators are jealous of our success, and they have convinced the body of senators to vote against me and revoke my governorship of Gaul."

An unpleasant murmur rose from the men, and Caesar waited for the clamor to subside.

"I have tried to convince Pompeius to renew our alliance and suggested that he marry my grandniece Octavia, but he refused and now even he opposes me. He tried to introduce a law which would have banned me from being elected as Consul unless I returned to Rome, but my friend, Scribonius Curius, a Tribune of the Plebeians, vetoed the law."

Several men shouted profanities about Pompeius, and the crowd was starting to roil. Caesar now had their attention and their loyalty confirmed, but he knew he needed to control their fervor.

"We still have many friends in Rome, and the people of Rome still favor me. To generate added support from the nobles, I am sending some of our leading men to Rome. Tribune Gnaeus, son of the influential statesman Gnaeus Domitius Ahenobarbus, will journey to the city with Legate Quintus Cicero, who, I am sure, can convince his older brother to join us. Aquila, who trained under Cicero, will also be one of our envoys."

The crowd of officers calmed and then cheered on the men designated by Caesar as their ambassadors. Like so many times in his speeches, Caesar worked the men's passions and minds as he proclaimed, "We will not be rash and heady like an immature and insecure man who thinks he must show force to prove himself. It is easier to find men who will volunteer to die than to find those who are willing to endure pain with patience. You have proven your steadiness and discipline in our Gallic campaign. While we do not want bloodshed, we will continue to train here and become stronger day by day. We will be ready for whatever happens!" Shouts of affirmation echoed through the evening air.

Early the next morning, Aquila, Gnaeus, and Quintus traveled rapidly east along the Via Domitia, their Sicilian-bred mounts quite comfortable to be trotting almost at their own will. After several hours, the men stopped to water their horses and take a break.

Quintus remarked, "Gnaeus, every time we pass another milepost I am reminded that this road was built under your grandfather's consulship. You come from a family with much history and fame."

"All Romans should be proud of their ancestors. Your brother is already a legend in the Senate. His tongue is sharper than a Roman sword," replied Gnaeus.

"Ha! Yes, that is right. He studied in Rhodes under the best Greek teachers, but my brother, known for his eloquence, has high regards for Caesar's discourses. When Caesar was young, he was also a student at Rhodes. Cicero declared that Caesar's style is elegant as well as transparent, even grand and in a sense noble. And my brother further embellished as he once said: 'What orator would you rank above him of those who have devoted themselves to nothing else? Who has cleverer or more frequent epigrams? Who is either more picturesque or choicer in diction?' Those were my brother Cicero's words. And think of our own experiences. We have had our spirits captured by Caesar as he has motivated us with speeches before a host of battles."

Aquila added, "Talking of our leader, I heard that as a young man reporting to his first duty as tribune in Narbo, Caesar made this same trip in seven days!" Aquila took three steps, vaulted into his saddle and urged his mount into a fast trot. He looked back at his companions and shouted, "We can beat his time! Vado!"

Over the next several days, they traveled rapidly along the paved Roman road. They passed from Narbonese Gaul into Cisalpine Gaul over the pass in the Alps where Hannibal had entered Italy hundreds of years before. The horses thrived on the motion. On the third night, the men sat around their campfire near an inn. After a quick meal, they were ready to sleep. Gnaeus lay on his stomach and pulled his wool blanket over his head as he said, "Four more days of this and I don't know if I will ever sleep on my backside again."

Quintus answered, "At least you can stay in Rome. Aquila and I must go halfway across the world to reach my brother in Cilicia."

Gnaeus quickly fell asleep and was soon breathing heavily. Aquila gazed into the fire and asked Quintus, "Why did your brother agree to take the governor's position? He once told me he did not regret leaving the military and would rather live in Rome working as an advocate supporting the Republic. I have never met a more honest and patriotic man."

Quintus stared into the flickering flames.

"Because he cares so much for Rome, he will subject himself to military duty. The province was on the verge of collapse before he arrived. After Crassus's defeat in the east, it appeared the Parthians would next invade the neighboring province of Cilicia. My brother's success was in part due to gaining the admiration of the people he governed. He did not increase their taxes to pay for the two legions he raised to defend them, but he procured the funds from wealthy Roman friends who had commercial investments in the province. He is proud of that. Proud not to make the people suffer."

Aquila and Quintus both sat silently for several minutes watching the flames.

"My tutor in Tauromenium also credited your brother with high moral standards. When he was the financial administrator for Sicily, the people respected him for his honesty and fairness. That is a hard and uncommon thing in our world," Aquila said.

"It is hard in any world," Quintus answered as he rolled over to sleep.

The next morning, they ate chunks of hard bread as they rolled up their blankets and continued their ride. Aquila felt the stiffness and pain fade away after the first few miles. They slowed down at the towns, including Genua, a city on the Tyrrhenian Sea which had originally been founded by native blond-haired Ligurians. When the Etruscans took control, they had developed the city into a thriving seaport while Rome was still a small town.

Just south of Genua, they stopped at a roadside tavern which was a rest stop for coaches. Behind the tavern were stables with horses available for the government postal express riders. It was noon on their sixth day out from Narbo. They stood street-side at the serving bar, which was made of stone with depressions carved into the counter to hold pasta (lagane), soups, stews, and sauces. They ordered fresh bread and cheese.

"I'll take a bowl of that soup you have there. I've had the red sauce before; that's a spicy fish sauce, right? But what is that green sauce?" Aquila asked of the bartender.

"You haven't been to Genua before or you would know that this sauce is a favorite around here. It is made from pine nuts and basil. You should try it. It is good with lagane or with bread."

Aquila glanced at his companions. Quintus's expression was nonjudgmental, but Gnaeus grimaced, indicating his disdain for the sauce. He would decide himself.

"I'll take some of the green sauce." They stood drinking the soup from small ceramic bowls. Aquila dipped a piece of bread into the sauce.

Quintus poured each of them some wine and added an equal amount of water. Aquila talked while chewing his bread.

"This is good sauce, but I would not eat it every day. Hey, what is with the water?"

Gnaeus raised his cup as if he were making a toast. The tone of his voice was aloof, but rich with conviviality.

"Friends, we definitely did not cut our rations of vinegar with water on the march. When we got back to Narbo, we had been away from real wine so long, we preferred not to cut our wine, to savor every drop at full strength. But we are heading back to civilization, to the city. We need to adjust our habits accordingly. Salute!"

It was less than an hour to sunset, and Gnaeus, riding in the front, pulled his horse to a stop. "We will need to ride tonight to beat Caesar's seven-day ride."

Aquila looked doubtful. "There is no moon. How will we see the road?"

"The horses have excellent night vision and will be able find their way down the road."

Quintus nodded.

Aquila spurred his horse ahead and shouted, "Gnaeus, you are the horse expert, so I will take your word!"

As the sun set, they continued to ride into the evening. After an hour of riding in the dark, they stopped at a creek to water the horses and rest. They could barely see each other or the road. As Aquila peered at the clear sky, he saw thousands of brilliant stars. Near the horizon was the brightest star blazing white, and overhead was a yellowish star almost as bright.

Quintus noticed Aquila's gaze and commented, "Which gods and goddesses are out tonight?"

Aquila answered, neither aware nor caring if Quintus's question was serious or not. "The brightest white one, the most beautiful one, is Venus and the one overhead is her father, Jupiter."

"You speak as if you believe in them. Do you?" Quintus asked.

"I have not decided yet. I do not sense their presence. Maybe I need to frequent their temples more often. In Sicily, many people pray to Vulcan, who they believe lives in Etna. I do feel the spirit of my mother and father. They are somehow with me, and I even feel the spirit of my grandparents, although they are no longer alive."

The timbre of Quintus's voice was sincere as he said, "Our family's primary devotion is to our ancestors. But when running for election, I know my brother had to show respect for as many deities and religious traditions as possible. Hey, Aquila, look— some god or something up there likes us. Here comes a half-moon rising to help light our way! Vado!"

It was late in the afternoon of the seventh day when they

reached Rome. They boarded their horses at a stable on the right bank of the Tiber River before crossing the bridge into the city. Aquila was so tired he barely heard Quintus tell him to meet at the stable in three days. They would ride to Brundisium and take a ship to Cilicia. Aquila and Gnaeus promised to connect in the future. He knew that Gnaeus, a patrician, had completed his short military calling and would begin his political career in politics in Rome. Aquila wondered if he would advocate political support for Caesar.

Aquila arrived at Cicero's house, eager to see Tullia. She was now between marriages after her divorce by Furius, and he assumed she would be there. Aquila knocked at the door. It was late and everyone was asleep in the household except the doorman, whose familiar face made Aquila nostalgic for his former nights out as a city boy. The guard whispered that Aquila's old room was empty. Aquila had barely removed his sandals when he fell back on the bed and soon was asleep. He slept soundly into the afternoon. A slave entered the room and carried a new tunic and a bowl of hot water. Aquila then joined Terentia and Tullia, who were getting ready for their evening meal.

Terentia seemed genuinely happy to see him. "Welcome back, soldier, or should I say, Centurion!"

Tullia, her face glowing, gave him a firm hug. Mother, he is a cavalry officer now! He is a tribune."

"Hmmm, then he can help me receive clients in the morning."

"Mistress, I wish I could help, but I must leave in two days for Cilicia."

The light in Tullia's eyes dimmed.

"I was just joking. What you can do is tell Cicero to come back to Rome. You must know that we are divorced. I don't miss him a bit, but his daughter does. He promised he would only serve as governor for one year," said Terentia. She directed her attention to her daughter. "Tullia, I have an appointment with friends at the baths. You stay with Lucius and keep him company."

The afternoon seemed like old times to Tullia and Aquila as they sat in the garden and conversed as if they had never parted. After their initial burst of excitement, their conversation slowed. The household slaves had gone to the market and a hush settled over the house. Aquila and Tullia sat quietly on a stone bench together, gazing out at the garden, the sound of the water splashing in the fountain. The marble columns of the portico surrounding the garden were a brilliant white in the warm sun.

Tullia scooted closer so their hips touched. She recited without looking at him: "*Turn, magic wheel, draw homeward him I love, May Aphrodite whirl him to my door!*–It worked. I prayed for you to come back."

"Yes, I came back, but whatever god or goddess you prayed to isn't very generous, only letting me stay for two days."

"Who is to stop you from staying longer?"

"It is my duty. I am still in the legions."

"You sound like my father talking now. But I guess that is not so bad."

"Besides, Tullia, Theocritus meant that verse to be for lovers, not friends."

"Best friends can be lovers."

"Yes, but . . . Tullia, we should not torture ourselves with something we cannot have."

Tullia gently took his hand and led him to his bedroom. Aquila awoke later that afternoon with Tullia's warm body pressed against him. It had been perfect. He was so content he did not want to ever move from her side.

Then he had a feeling that this had happened before and he jerked upright. "Wake up! Your mother!"

Tullia pulled him back down and whispered, "Don't worry, the doorman would have warned us. He is loyal to me and I know you two are comrades."

Calmed, his thoughts traveled back to three years before. "It was you, that night, here in this room! Tullia, why did you make it happen that way?"

"I am sorry you didn't know it was me. I was determined that you would be my first. That way I would know the difference from being with a man I loved versus a man I was forced to marry. And again today, it was wonderful. We were both completely aware, so we will remember each other. One time with you is better than a lifetime with other men. We may not ever have another chance. In several weeks, I am obligated to marry again for the family."

Aquila was reassured that Tullia had remained strong and had kept her self-respect despite her hardships. He joined her in facing the inevitable, which they could not change. He did not question her anymore, but said, "My love, I can see that I am not the only one who is bound by duty."

6 CILICIA

Aquila and Quintus retrieved their horses from the stables and headed south from Rome along the Via Appia. They stopped at inns overnight and completed the 300 mile journey in a week. On the seventh day, they arrived in the city of Brundisium, the seaport that linked Italy to the eastern Mediterranean. The men gained passage on a ship which was outfitted to transport their horses as well. The horses were loaded through a door in the hull of the large sailing ship. Below deck were stalls with slings to support the horses in case of rough seas.

The ship crossed the Adriatic Sea to Greece, hugged the Greek coast, and stopped over at the port of Piraeus, which served Athens. After crossing the Aegean Sea, they arrived at the seaport of Tarsus, the capital of the Roman province of Cilicia. The city was well known for its Greek culture and was home to many scholars of philosophy and literature.

#

After almost two weeks on the sea, Quintus and Aquila were both glad to be on dry land at Cicero's residence in Tarsus. This morning, they waited for Cicero to take a recess from his morning business. Aquila watched his former mentor with some curiosity. Instead of the calm and unhurried man he remembered in Rome, he now observed a man rapidly planning, making decisions, and giving orders to couriers and tribunes passing in and out of his office. Cicero explained that he had planned on being in Cilicia for one year and he was determined to achieve his goal of stabilizing the province before departing.

Aquila, still respectful of his "second" father Cicero, but now with more confidence and experience, decided to suggest some advice.

"Your brother and I are both committed to helping you meet your goals so you can return to Rome and make the most of your influence. Caesar needs your help in Rome."

Cicero assessed his brother and Aquila.

"His charisma has worked on you, too, hasn't it? Caesar has convinced you he is the one, the savior of the people. He is very intelligent, but his proposals are too good to be true."

Knowing that Cicero was a genuine patriot and worked tirelessly to help the people, Aquila countered, "Caesar's proposed laws will benefit the common people, and he has worked to re-establish the power of the plebeians' tribunes."

"Caesar's reforms will not last. Everything he does is intended to increase his power. The Senate will undermine all his actions because Caesar tries to push too far. He knows no compromise. His talent for speed and surprise in battle is genius, but politically he will not survive. He expects everyone to obey and agree with him," said Cicero.

Aquila knew from experience Caesar's tactics in war and assumed they would make him successful in his quest for power.

"If I had to choose one man to rule, it would be Caesar; he has the energy and foresight."

Cicero's voice softened.

"I am passionate about this subject and organized my thoughts by writing *De Re Publica*, which I will publish when I return to Rome. Let me remind you that our forefathers created the Republic to ensure that one man does not acquire too much power. The power of the head of state has been divided between the two consuls, one a plebeian and the other a patrician. Since their terms are only for one year, this further limits accumulation of power. Combined with the veto power of the plebeian tribunes and their ability to propose laws to protect the people, Rome has remained strong as a republic for almost five hundred years. I do not see Caesar supporting the Republican constitution."

Aquila answered, "Caesar has pardoned countrymen whom he has defeated, unlike the dictatorships of Marius and Sulla. They conscripted and slaughtered their political opponents."

"But what will happen after he is gone? Caesar's ambition may destroy the already weakened republic and consolidate the power. Then other rulers following him who are corrupt and unpatriotic will benefit from the path he has blazed."

"Will you consider joining Caesar?" Aquila asked.

"I will not throw everything in with Caesar, son. If he relinquishes the command of his legions to the Senate and returns to Rome to work out a peaceful resolution, he will have my support."

Cicero paused when a servant arrived carrying a tray of food and drink. As Cicero handed Quintus and Aquila each a cup of wine, he smiled and said,

"Let's talk of something more pleasant. How was your visit with Tullia?"

#

The next day Cicero, Quintus, and Aquila, leading a century of Roman cavalry, rode north of Tarsus through wide and fertile plains of sesame, barley, wheat, and millet. Late in the afternoon they entered the green foothills of the Taurus Mountains and approached the Roman military camp. The camp was located south of the mountain pass called the Cilician Gates, through which threaded an ancient trade route. The garrison was comprised of three legions: an Italian legion which Cicero had brought with him and two additional legions that he had raised from the local population. He had equipped and trained the new recruits in the same manner as the traditional Roman legionaries.

As they neared the main gate of the camp, they returned the guards' brisk chorus.

"Virtus!"

They dismounted and entered the headquarters tent. Cicero nodded at his brother.

"Quintus, you have more experience as a legate than anyone in Cilicia. As we discussed, you will replace me as supreme commander. The legate of each legion will report to you. That should be an easy transition. Today we will meet with them as well as the senior cavalry commander.

"Aquila, you will lead the cavalry cohort assigned to the Twenty-Second Legion, consisting primarily of Pontians. I am confident the men will quickly accept your leadership. Most of Caesar's legions were Italian or Roman Spaniards and all spoke Latin, but here you will find a more international group of soldiers. All the officers and centurions speak Latin, but you will hear them using Greek with the men and you will also hear some legionaries speaking in a Celtic tongue."

Surprised, Aquila was about to question Cicero, but Quintus asked first.

"Celtic? Do you mean the language of Gaul?"

"Yes, there is a tribe in this region whose people are called Galatians. According to the Galatian legends, their ancestors migrated from Gaul many generations ago. They speak Celtic, but many also speak Greek, because they lived near the Greek city-states for so long. So now, you are going to fight alongside Celts rather than against them. As you know, like their western brethren, they are ferocious fighters."

Aquila was interested in meeting the Galatian legionaries. He noticed some had their left earlobes pierced with small jeweled earrings, reflecting a familiar green sparkle. He introduced himself to a group of the legionaries. As he was about to inquire regarding their earrings, one of the men voiced, "We noticed your ring with the green garnet. And sir . . . your name . . . I am wondering about the similarity to the name of our country. Did you know that the green garnet is revered in Pontus?"

"The ring was given to me by my father in Sicily. I have noticed your earrings are also fitted with green garnets. My father told me green garnets are found north of the Black Sea. According to the family legend, our ancestors came from the east, across the sea. Maybe it was the Black Sea," Aquila said.

Aquila's last statement further sparked the imagination of

the Pontian legionaries. Before Aquila returned to Tarsus, rumor had already spread that Aquila was from an ancient Pontus family.

#

Spring was turning to summer in the year the consuls Lepidus Paullus and G. Claudius Marcellus Minor served. Cicero prepared to return to Rome, satisfied with his brother's command of the legions. Aquila stood on the dock in Tarsus and surveyed the river port lined with troop transports. Now that the province was at peace, Cicero would take the Italian legion back to Italy, leaving the two allied legions to garrison Cilicia. Several of the transports had already weighed anchor and had begun drifting downriver toward the sea. Cicero was happy to be heading home and was in a joyous mood as he embraced Quintus and Aquila in farewell.

"Brother, you will make a good governor. And don't worry, I will push the Senate to replace you soon."

Aquila handed Cicero a small pouch with a letter and some incense for Tullia.

"Aquila, your letter and gift will lift her spirits. We all grieved for Tullia after her son died a few weeks after birth. But her husband Dolabella was not supportive of her in her misery. He expressed only disappointment in the death of his son and showed no concern for her welfare. You, more than anyone, can help her. Please write to her. It is good I am returning, as I think Terentia will not take her back if she divorces again. I know Cilicia will be in good hands with you and Quintus. When I return to Rome, I will be sitting among turbulent sessions at the Senate. But my skills will be more useful in Rome than in Cilicia. Remember, when you govern, the well-being of the people is the supreme law."

#

Months later, on a day in late February, in the year Claudius Marcellus and Cornelius Lentulus COS, Quintus called Aquila to his office.

"A letter has just arrived from Cicero. The Senate ordered that Julius Caesar disband his army or be declared an enemy of the state. But Caesar, in his characteristic lightning speed, crossed the Rubicon River and threatened Rome before the Senate could organize a proper defense. Pompeius, caught unprepared, fled Italy and joined his legions across the Adriatic Sea in Illyria. Many of the Senators followed Pompeius, including Cicero. I will be leaving tomorrow to join my brother."

Aquila was not surprised that Quintus was in support of Pompeius. Quintus handed Aquila the letter. After reading the details, Aquila asked, "Cicero states in his letter that Pompeius had Caesar outnumbered two to one in Italy. Caesar had only one legion with him. Why didn't Pompeius engage Caesar?"

"We both served under Caesar. He was always outnumbered, yet his unexpected tactics confused the enemy. How can you forget the agony of all the forced marches? And his uncanny ability to use the right strategy at the right time against the right foe? He is a military genius and although he can be reckless, he is also lucky. A religious person would say he has the gods on his side.

"Aquila, I must go to Illyria. There Pompeius will combine the Italian legions with his veteran legions. Caesar will find himself outnumbered three or even four to one, but they will be Roman troops, not barbarians."

"You are right, Quintus. I think our odds are good with Pompeius. Of course, I am coming with you."

"There will be no senior officers staying with the garrison in Cilicia. Aquila, the Republic needs you here. With the Senate in flight there is not time nor manpower to assign a new governor to Cilicia. As for me, my first loyalty is to my brother, but I strongly agree with his firm belief in the republican constitution. The Parthians know Rome is in turmoil and are just waiting for the chance to invade. Cicero did a masterful job in restoring the province and winning the hearts of the people here. You would do him a great honor in preserving what he accomplished. I am confident that with your leadership the auxiliary legions will remain loyal and will keep Cilicia secure."

"Then I will stay, Quintus. Your brother has been like a father to me."

During the next month, Aquila became concerned about the civil war developing in northern Greece and Illyria. The military mail was no longer being delivered to Cilicia, and the winter curtailment of sea travel further curbed communications. He increased the frequency and size of his patrols east and north of Cilicia to discourage incursions, and he ensured they were visible as a show of force to dispel rumor that the Roman garrison had pulled out to fight in the civil war.

In the vacuum created by the civil war, Aquila was promoted to Legate. His personality was such that he could get along with almost anyone, and he motivated men to follow his lead. Like Caesar, he spent much of his time at the campfires and baths developing relationships with his men.

Merchants returning from the kingdom north of the Taurus Mountains spread word that Pharnaces, King of Pontus, was planning to invade Cilicia. Aquila hoped to avoid a war, or at least delay hostilities. He knew he would not get reinforcements in the near future. He decided to lead a delegation to parley with

Pharnaces. Learning that Pharnaces was rather vain, adored lavishness, and was proud of his noble status, Aquila wore a brilliant white tunic. He had his men's armor polished to exceptional brilliance and dressed his men's mounts in colorful trimmings of the type favored by the native nobility. Aquila intended to impress and honor Pharnaces by appearing as dignified as possible.

The province of Pontus had been acquired by Rome twenty years earlier. Pharnaces's father, Mithridates, had been defeated by Pompeius, who had rewarded his veteran legionaries with land at the site of the battle. There they had founded the city of Nicopolis, "City of Victory." In their meeting at Zela, Aquila reminded Pharnaces peace and prosperity had been maintained since his kingdom and Rome had become allies twenty years earlier. Aquila promised Pharnaces there would be increased grain trade with Pontus and special protection for merchants from Pontus traveling to the east through Cilicia. The conference was genial, and Pharnaces referred to the affable Aquila as his "Pontian brother, the Roman who possesses the green garnet." Aquila's strategy had worked, but he was fearful he would not be able to hold Cilicia without help.

Several weeks after his meeting with Pharnaces, Aquila relaxed in the provincial governor's house in Tarsus. It was a cool spring morning and he had finished breakfast. He gazed north from the portico across the plains toward the impressive snowcapped mountains. *Those peaks are the Taurus Mountains. What a coincidence. Tauromenium, where I studied in Sicily, was named after the slope of Mount Taurus. That is where I met Tullia... I miss her so much!*

His thoughts were interrupted by his doorman.

"Legate, a merchant from Pontus has requested a reception

and waits outside your office."

Aquila felt uncomfortable sitting in a Curule Chair, the Romans' traditional seat of authority. However, he understood that in his role he must employ the accoutrements of the governor. He did not wear a toga, but put on his best tunic and a bright red cloak. His lower legs were exposed, revealing his muscular calves, hardened from years of training and countless miles of marching.

When the visitor entered the receiving hall, Aquila saw a young man dressed in native attire. He wore loose trousers, a shirt overlaid by the leather vest worn by travelers, and a dull red turban. Various articles protruded from the vest pockets, among them a pair of dagger handles. The caller approached Aquila with self-assurance and stood quietly before him. Aquila was puzzled why the doorman had let in a boy and why an adolescent was asking for an audience. The visitor spoke.

"Proconsul, thank you for receiving me. May I make my request?"

Aquila then determined the visitor was actually a woman and wondered why she would be here without her husband or father as an escort. His thoughts cascaded from one disposition to another until he imagined that she must be attractive, even under those baggy men's clothes.

Aquila blinked and sat speechless. He was captivated by her dark eyes and particularly enraptured by the way her lips moved when she talked. Neither the guards standing at ready, nor the scribe, nor the tribune sitting nearby revealed any signs that they sensed Aquila's perplexity. The visitor also stood patiently waiting for Aquila's response. He realized he had not listened to a word she had said and stammered, "Do you speak Greek, um, uh, miss?"

She looked puzzled, but her voice did not betray any emotion.

"I did speak Greek, Proconsul."

Aquila was tantalized. He was captivated by her seductive lips and failed to register what she had said.

"Yes, of course. What did you say?"

"Proconsul, my father, Poleman, is sick. He has collapsed in your anteroom and is so weak that he is unable to appeal to you for help. We are wool merchants from Zela. My father cannot make the journey home without care. No one in Tarsus will guide us to a physician."

Aquila stood, directed his guards to assist her father to a spare bedroom, and called for his servants to bring water. He had the tribune send for one of the legion's physicians, although it would be late afternoon before he arrived. When the merchant's daughter was sure her father was as comfortable as possible in a spare bedroom, she left one of the household slaves to cool his fever with wet cloths.

She joined Aquila in the peristylium at the center of the house. Slaves served them nuts and olives. They sat in the garden sipping wine.

"Thank you, Proconsul, for helping my father."

"I have summoned a physician from the Twenty-Second Legion. He is also a Pontian, I believe of Greek descent." He waited, wondering if she would comment, as he was interested in her background. *Is she Greek, Asian, Armenian?* She did not comment or show any expression.

"Young lady, titles are not really important to me, but the

Senate has not replaced Proconsul Cicero and in the interim I am fulfilling the post. I am the Roman Legate of this province. But please, let's not be formal. Call me Aquila."

"As you wish, and please call me Miriam."

Neither talked much as they sampled the fare and sipped wine. Several times a messenger or tribune arrived and Aquila briefly left the room to conduct business.

Although her glass of wine was half full and most of the food was still on her plate, Miriam stood.

"I must check on my father. Also, our horses and goods are unattended in the street."

"No, I . . . I mean, of course, you are concerned for your father. My staff is taking good care of him, and I had your horse and pack mules brought into the stables. They are secure."

Miriam paused and stared coolly at Aquila. He felt self-conscious, but caught himself and confirmed, "Yes, yes, please attend to your father."

She turned and retreated to her father's room.

As she left, Aquila wondered, *Why am I so fixated with her? I have never been unnerved in battle, but her presence stresses me. She is the steady one.*

In the evening, Miriam declined an invitation to dine with Aquila. The physician arrived and she remained with her father during his examination. The next morning, her father's fever had broken. Poleman was still rather weak, but they thanked Aquila and planned to continue their trip back to Pontus, north through the Taurus Mountains.

After they had left, Aquila questioned the physician.

"Dioscorides, what did you do to cure him so fast? The merchant had a terrible fever."

"Wine and water mixed with the herb borage. It is excellent for fevers. It is called the warriors' wine. Pontian soldiers tend to drink it for courage before battle. It is also good for depression."

"Hmm, where did you learn about this herb?"

"My father was a military physician in the army of King Mithridates. He learned from Master Krateuas, a Greek Pontian. He left me a copy of Krateuas's book on herbs and remedies. I am teaching my son, Pedianus, from the master's book."

"Thank you, Dioscorides. I am also interested in anything Poleman or Miriam said while you were with them that may be useful."

"Useful, Legate?"

"Did they say anything about King Pharnaces or the situation in Pontus?"

"No. But I am quite surprised Miriam asked for your help. She told me her mother and brothers died in the wars against Rome. And then to my surprise, her father said when he got back to Zela, he would have good things to say about a Roman for the first time in his life."

\#

Poleman's trade route was to Syria and back to Pontus through the Cilician Gates, taking advantage of the Roman peace in the province and the Roman roads. He stopped with Miriam in Tarsus on their first return trip after his sickness. Aquila invited

Poleman, Miriam, and her male cousins traveling with them to lunch at the governor's residence.

As they relaxed on couches in the bright sunlight of the peristylium, Poleman smiled as he said, "Miriam is just as headstrong as her mother. She decided that her father would not take care of himself, so she must travel with me on my trading expeditions."

Poleman glanced at Miriam, who showed no reaction when he said, "This has made it impractical for her to consider a traditional marriage. I must say she is an excellent wool merchant, although she has taken on an unusual role for a woman."

Aquila had looked forward to seeing Miriam again and he was enchanted just watching her enjoy her food and drink. She, however, showed no signs of interest in him.

#

In September, C. Julius Caesar II and P. Servilius Vatia Isauricus COS, news arrived from Illyria of two battles between Pompeius's and Caesar's forces. For weeks Caesar's army had followed on the heels of Pompeius's legions, trying to lure them into a disadvantageous location. Pompeius had countered by avoiding battle. His ships controlled the sea lanes from Italy and kept Caesar's troops in the field without the ability to resupply. Then Labienus, Caesar's second in command at Alesia, deserted him and joined Pompeius. Encouraged by this defection, Pompeius's legions turned on Caesar's army. At the Battle of Dyrrhacium, although Caesar's troops were defeated, they were able to retreat effectively and regroup.

Pompeius followed to finish off Caesar, but did not know Antonius Marcus had crossed the Adriatic Sea and had arrived with supplies and reinforcements. At Pharsalus, Caesar's outnumbered forces soundly defeated Pompeius's army. Pompeius fled to Egypt and remnants of the senate that had opposed Caesar regrouped at the city-state of Utica in North Africa.

Aquila could not obtain any information about Cicero or Quintus in the confusion and turmoil that followed the decisive battle. However, in January Q. Calenus and P. Vatinius COS, Caesar arrived in Tarsus with the Thirty-Sixth and Sixth legions. The Thirty-Sixth, made up of veterans from Pompeius's defeated army, had changed allegiance after the Battle of Pharsalus.

Aquila entered Caesar's headquarters at his camp north of Tarsus. He was quickly reminded of Caesar's dynamic personality. He reviewed troop strength, dictated instructions to his scribe for distribution to staff officers and at the same time discussed with Aquila his plans for the eastern Roman provinces.

"Aquila, you have served well and kept the province intact. I have appointed Legate Domitius Calvinus as new provincial governor, but I cannot grant your request to rejoin the Sixth when we go to Egypt. Your experience here is too valuable and Calvinus will need your guidance. I am leaving the Thirty-Sixth here, and I'm sailing to Egypt with the Sixth in a few days. I have reports that Pompeius is in Egypt under King Ptolemy's protection."

Aquila, disappointed he was not assigned to the Sixth, thought of challenging Caesar. He deserved to go with his comrades. But as thoughts of Miriam slipped in, he simply answered, "Yes, sir." He saluted with a strong "Virtus!" Turning to leave, he added, "Caesar, can you tell me anything about Cicero and Quintus?"

Aquila smiled and now gave his total attention to Aquila.

"You will be pleased to know that both are back in Rome serving the Republic with my unconditional and complete pardon."

As he left Caesar's command tent, Aquila could hardly believe the news. He was ecstatic. *Not only have Cicero and Quintus survived the battles, but they are well and have been pardoned by Caesar!* Outside Caesar's tent, he encountered Pavius, the senior centurion, who had been his first mentor, and Primus Pilus of the Sixth.

"Pavius!"

They embraced and pounded each other on the back, unabashed with emotion. Pavius released his firm clinch and stepped back, still beaming with excitement. "Tribune, or should I say Legate? I know you can fill whatever role is demanded of you. How are you doing?"

"Excellent! It is good to see your familiar face, Pavius, but I will not be coming with you to Egypt. Before you leave, we must share some wine. I want to hear about Pharsalus!"

After Pavius finished his story of the battle, he appeared grim. He readily acknowledged they would get together later. Aquila left the camp and rode back to Tarsus to prepare his move out of the governor's house.

When he entered the atrium, Miriam was waiting. "I was told you were to leave in a few days with the Sixth Legion."

"No, I am staying in Cilicia, but I have been replaced as governor. Whatever assistance you may need, I can help you in that capacity for only one more day. Calvinus will move here tomorrow."

The expression on her face, usually emotionless, revealed faint signs of surprise and relief.

Aquila glanced around the atrium. "Where is your father?"

"He is fine, at home. He has decided that the traveling has become too hard for him."

"You cannot be traveling alone?"

"No, I have a handful of men with me, assistants, and cousins. They are playing dice with some of your men and will sleep in the stables with our horses and goods. Tomorrow I will need to return north. I have brought some marvelous Pontian wine I would like to share with you."

The next day the sun was already high when Aquila awoke. The fog in his head brought back memories of younger days when he had reveled late at night and had enjoyed too much wine. Memories of those days of lovemaking late into the night surfaced, and he smiled to himself. *Where is she? Where is Miriam? She seduced me last night. Where is that beautiful vixen?*

#

A few days later, the Sixth Legion, its strength down to four cohorts, about two thousand infantry, mustered in Tarsus and prepared to board ships to Egypt. Aquila and Pavius drank wine and traded war stories at a riverfront tavern. Then Pavius's smile faded and his voice was hushed and secretive.

"Watch out for yourself. This civil war is evil. Romans killing Romans. Caesar could have avoided this war. Before we fought Pompeius, I thought my deep loyalty to Caesar would overcome my disdain for killing other Romans. During battle, you fight without much thought. As soldiers, we are conditioned to seeing piles of bodies after a battle, but not Romans killed by fellow Romans, some who I even knew when we served together. It is not right. I am relieved we are going to Egypt."

Pavius took a long drink of wine and continued, "Aquila, the legions are my career. But to most men, it is a temporary life. To quell their disloyalty, Caesar promised most of the Ninth and Tenth legions huge rewards and a discharge once they defeated Pompeius. But he did not keep his promise. They were on the verge of revolt. Caesar handled the discord in these legions by having them take the prisoners and booty back to Rome with a promise that he would join them after he captured Pompeius. So, to you I advise, stay aware and take care of yourself."

#

Calvinus and Aquila worked closely together the next few months to organize their forces. The veteran legionaries of the Thirty-Sixth Legion organized and trained a new legion, the Second Cilician. The Twenty-Second Legion absorbed what was left of the First Cilician, which had been organized by Cicero. These three legions of infantry were supported by a cohort of Roman cavalry led by Aquila. His days were demanding and his daydreams of Miriam faded.

King Pharnaces discovered that Caesar had departed. He seized the opportunity and began a campaign to retake those lands which had once belonged to his father's kingdom. When Pharnaces's forces surrounded Zela, Calvinus decided to intervene. He led the Roman army north and built a fortified camp within several miles of the besieged city. Aquila scouted ahead with the cavalry to determine the location and strength of the Pontian army. He arrived at the edge of a rocky flatland where the hilltop city of Zela came into view. Aquila recognized Pharnaces's leading general, Noacedes, at the head of several score of mounted soldiers blocking the road. The general hailed Aquila by name and requested to talk under truce.

"My Roman friend, why do you need to build a fortified camp? We enjoyed your company on your previous diplomatic visits. You are considered a friend and ally of King Pharnaces."

"Why does Pharnaces send troops to Bithynia and now threaten Zela?" Aquila countered.

"We heard of the reduction of Roman troops. The king is acting as a good and true ally to Rome by defending the province until Caesar returns."

"I am confident Rome can keep this region secure. As a representative of Caesar and Rome, I call for the withdrawal of your troops. According to the treaty negotiated by Pompeius and your grandfather, Zela is not part of the region that you govern in Rome's name."

Noacedes answered, "If it were anyone else, I would be risking my life taking that kind of demand back to my king. But for you, Aquila, I will do it. I will report your wishes to King Pharnaces and give you his answer here tomorrow, shortly after sunrise."

The next morning the sun had just climbed above the horizon as Aquila arrived at the meeting place with Noacedes. The Pontian sat beside a small fire roasting nuts. Aquila dismounted and enjoyed the familiar aroma of hot hazelnuts. He addressed his counterpart.

"General, that wonderful smell makes me remember my home. My family grows hazelnuts in Sicily."

Pharnaces smiled, then tossed a nut to Aquila. "You call these hazelnuts? The Greeks call them Pontic nuts. They grow in plenty along the shores of the Black Sea. We have such a surplus. We export shiploads to Greece. Anyway, they are very tasty. Join me for some breakfast and we will talk."

Warmed by the fire, they cracked and ate hazelnuts and drank from Aquila's water skin.

"Has your king considered our proposal?"

"Yes, yes. Your three legions are proof Rome can keep Pontus secure. We are breaking camp now. By the time we finish breakfast, our army will be returning east."

Calvinus decided to follow with his legions to make sure they left the region. During the next weeks, the Romans followed the Pontian army eastward. Pharnaces did not appear to be in a hurry. Roman supplies were running low. Calvinus made the decision to resupply at the Hellenic city of Nicopolis. The city had been originally settled sixteen years earlier by a mixture of retired Roman soldiers and local peasants, commemorating Pompeius's victory over King Mithridates of Pontus. Calvinus expected the people there would be friendly.

Aquila led his cavalry as he reconnoitered ahead of the marching infantry. As they approached the city, Aquila observed Nicopolis was situated at the base of a heavily forested mountain bordered by a well-watered, fertile plain covered in fields of kamut, camel's tooth wheat. The Pontian army had passed by the city and bivouacked about a half mile east of Nicopolis, to rest before they advanced to the mountain pass. The gates of Nicopolis were open, activity seemed normal, and nothing was judged suspicious. Aquila sent a tribune and a squad of soldiers to enter the city and negotiate for supplies.

The tribune returned shortly. "Sir, the city magistrate was cooperative and is already collecting supplies for us."

A Roman scout soon returned and reported to Aquila, "The

Pontians stopped for their midday meal next to the river."

"Tell Proconsul Calvinus the situation here. I will be in the city organizing the supplies," Aquila said.

Aquila dismounted at the gate and led his horse into the city. His men did the same and followed. The townspeople suddenly disappeared into their shops and houses. A man shouted just before he slammed his door, "Romans, leave the city, quickly. Your enemies lie in wait!"

Those remaining on the street drew weapons and began to rush the dismounted Romans. Aquila shouted back to his men behind him:

"Go back! Ambush!"

He vaulted onto his horse, quickly took the reins, urging his horse into a gallop, and followed his men speeding toward the gate. Men brandishing spears forced several of the horses to stop. Riders fell to the ground and some were dragged from their saddles as armed men swarmed onto the legionaries. Aquila rode forward, but a cart rolled into his path. His horse reared up, throwing him off. As his head hit the ground, a halo of gray formed in his field of vision, receding until his sight contracted into a pinpoint of light, and then everything went black.

7 ZELA

When he regained consciousness, Aquila's hands were tied behind his back and a heavy rope collar hung around his neck. He had slept among a pile of men, several from his cohort, bound in the same fashion. He was throttled from the strong odor of sweat, blood, and urine.

"Get up! Get up or we'll leave you here to die!" a voice yelled in heavily accented Greek.

Aquila's head was foggy and heavy. His mouth was dry and his lips cracked. He was pulled to his feet as the string of prisoners struggled to stand. Aquila barely managed, unsteady on his feet. The line of men began to move and Aquila stumbled along. *What happened? How long have I been out?*

For the prisoners, the days that followed were uncountable. Walk on command, sit down, stand up, and walk again. Day after day. Aquila was so weak and tired he had no firm perception of reality. The prisoners were not fed. Water was poured into their mouths during stops. When they halted at villages and towns, men were detached from the line and sold as slaves. One evening, a guard stuffed a piece of bread in Aquila's mouth and whispered, "Hang on. You're too valuable to die."

The guard showed him that he had Aquila's green garnet ring. "I know who you are, and you will bring a large ransom."

The next morning when Aquila awoke, the pangs of hunger were less. *Was that a dream? The conversation with the guard? But I can still taste the bread! There is the guard now. Yes, it did happen. I can tell by the way he made eye contact.*

#

Late in the next day, the column of prisoners stopped. Aquila looked ahead across the dry plain and recognized the city of Zela, high on a rocky hill. They dragged themselves up a long ridge and entered the city. The guard who had fed Aquila cut him from the line of prisoners and pushed him into a side alley.

Aquila heard a loud voice bellow, "Stop him. That is one I bought."

A townsman, attired in elegant clothes and escorted by two men, grabbed him by the rope around his neck. The bodyguards drew daggers and held Aquila. Their master looked back and said, "I already paid you . . ." He stopped as he realized the guard that delivered Aquila had disappeared.

Miriam appeared in the alley, blocking the group's access to the main street. She spoke in her composed tone.

"I have already paid for this slave. Untie him and leave."

"Oh, here is little Miriam, the trader's whelp, who acts like a man. I think you have been tricked."

Miriam stood silent, unmoving, and relaxed. Her arms hung loosely at her sides.

"Little lady, no one will believe you paid for him. You did not go through the proper channels. I have the papers here. So where is your courage without your army of cousins?" The man laughed and his servants joined in.

Miriam did not answer. Then she appeared worried as her eyes darted back and forth to a spot behind them. The men glanced back and she sprang forward, a dagger already in each hand, hidden by her sleeves.

Aquila, almost unconscious from his ordeal, detected only a blur of movement. He felt blood splatter on his face. The body guards clutched their forearms pressing the deep slashes on their wrists. The clatter of metal on stones sounded as their daggers dropped to the bloody pavement.

#

Aquila awoke after sleeping into the late afternoon. He recognized Poleman across the room. His first words reflected his greatest concern.

"Where is Miriam?"

"She is fine. And you? You have slept for over a day." Miriam's father carried a cup as he crossed the room to Aquila's bed and gave him some diluted wine to drink.

As Aquila tried to sit up, he let out a groan.

"Oh, my head!" He lay back and let out a long breath.

"Here is your ring."

Aquila looked puzzled.

"Yes, you are lucky. I have contacts across many provinces, including many slave brokers. I paid your ransom. Since

Nicopolis you have been marked to be delivered to me, but it appears you were sold twice."

Aquila slipped the ring on his finger next to the iron ring which signified his Roman citizenship.

"That woman! Uh, I mean your daughter. She is fearless. But why did she interfere and risk getting killed?"

"She shows such fierce commitment only to members of her family." Poleman chuckled as he whispered, "She was unaware that I ensured her cousins were nearby, just in case.

"Years ago, she overheard me when I told her mother that I wished she had been born a boy. I do regret saying that, let alone thinking it. However, she has never given me a clue that she felt unloved. Of course, she has made me proud of her a thousand times over."

The men were silent for several minutes.

"Aquila, Miriam is pregnant. The child is yours."

#

Over the next few days, Miriam spent only short periods with Aquila to ensure he was recovering. When she heard Pharnaces was returning to Zela, Poleman provided Aquila with a horse. Miriam arranged for escorts to go with Aquila to join the Roman survivors retreating from the Battle of Nicopolis.

As Aquila was about to leave, Miriam embraced him firmly and kissed him.

"Good bye, Aquila."

Why hasn't she told me herself she is pregnant?

"Yes, for now, Miriam, but I will be back."

Aquila departed and joined the troops retreating through the Cilician Gate. His horse trudged along the road as he gazed along the dry valley. *I lost Tullia. Now I have lost Miriam.*

#

Over the next few weeks, Aquila recovered in the Roman camp in Cilicia. One afternoon as he practiced vaults onto the wooden horse, he was surprised when he heard Pavius's familiar voice.

"Those jumps would not have reached the saddle on an Egyptian horse. They have some Arabian horses that make ours look like ponies!"

Aquila, sweating profusely, hugged his comrade as he said, "You are back! And the Sixth is back?"

"Yes, and I am one of the lucky ones. We lost many comrades. The legion has been reduced to barely two cohorts."

"Did Caesar catch Pompeius in Egypt? What happened?"

"When we arrived at the court of Ptolemy, the king of Egypt, Caesar inquired of Pompeius's whereabouts. Ptolemy presented the severed head of Pompeius, assuming Caesar would be pleased. Caesar was livid and I thought he was going to assault Ptolemy. But we had only one century and the rest of the legionaries were on the ships at anchor in the harbor. He turned on his heel and stomped back to our ship. As he passed, I could see he was shedding tears of fury. We returned to the fleet and sailed a few miles down the coast. Caesar was contacted by Ptolemy's sister, Cleopatra, who also claimed the throne of Egypt. Caesar became romantically involved with her. Allied with her troops, we defeated Ptolemy and Caesar placed

Cleopatra as ruler of Egypt."

"Ha, I am not surprised Caesar got sidetracked with a woman. You mean the Sixth didn't tramp into Alexandria singing their favorite marching song? 'Hide your wives, hide your women; the bald-headed debaucher is coming!'" said Aquila.

Pavius laughed. "Of course, Cleopatra is not just any woman. She was the key to Egypt as well as a very attractive woman. She used Caesar and vice versa. He would not even pry himself away from her when we heard about your loss at Nicopolis. But when word arrived that Roman citizens had been massacred and enslaved, he promptly returned to punish Pharnaces."

"Pavius, I missed all the excitement in Egypt, but I almost met my end at Nicopolis. I also fell for a woman, and she saved my life." They crossed the camp and stopped at the mess hall to relax and drink.

After Aquila described his ordeal to his friend, Pavius said, "Caesar wants to take full advantage of your experience here and your past experiences with the Sixth. The legionaries remember you for saving the legion's sacred standard at Gergovia. To help raise the spirits of the Sixth, he has assigned me to train you to be Primus Pilus of the Sixth Legion."

Within several days, Caesar held a staff meeting with his officers, including Pavius and Aquila.

"Calvinus, you were impatient at Nicopolis. The two Cilicia legions have lost too many men. I believe Pharnaces planned for the battle to be at Nicopolis. Yes, yes, because that was the location where his father, Mithridates, was defeated by Pompeius twenty years ago! With this temporary victory, Pharnaces has gained much confidence."

Caesar paced back and forth as he continued to harangue Calvinus.

"And now at Zela, he is fortifying his position at the same place the Pontians defeated a Roman army a generation ago. To him, it is fate. There is no stronger motivation than when one believes he is fulfilling a path destined by the gods. I am concerned this could become a long campaign and we will be lucky if we complete it by the end of the summer."

A tribune entered the command tent and interrupted Caesar's lecture.

"Consul, there are ambassadors from King Pharnaces here to see you."

"Bring them in, Tribune."

Two men entered and set a wooden chest on the ground in front of Caesar. They opened it to reveal a golden crown. Caesar's eyes stayed on the ambassadors as if the gift did not exist.

One of the men addressed Caesar in Greek, "May I read our king's message, Consul?"

Caesar affirmed the request with a nod.

"Exalted First Consul of the Roman Republic, Subjugator of Gaul and Egypt, I entreat that Caesar will not come as an enemy conqueror: I will submit to all your commands. I have erred and I promise Pontus will comply with all the conditions of the treaty with the Roman Senate."

"That's it?" Caesar answered smartly.

"Yes, Consul."

"Return to Pharnaces and tell him that I will grant clemency if he leaves Pontus, releases all Roman prisoners, and pays for all the destruction he has committed, as well as a ten-thousand-denarii tribute."

Caesar sent away the ambassadors and turned to Calvinus and Aquila.

"I want the army marching to Zela tomorrow morning."

The legions marched north through the Cilician Gates to Pontus the next day.

#

On a hot dry August afternoon after a long day's march though the rugged hills and valleys of the Taurus Mountains, Caesar surveyed the army of King Pharnaces. It was positioned about a half mile away on a ridge leading to the hilltop town of Zela. A valley separated the Roman legions and the Pontian fortified camp. Caesar took advantage of the terrain and constructed the Roman camp on the opposite side of the valley. Several cohorts stood ready in their armor as the fortified camp was being constructed. Caesar commented as he and Calvinus surveyed the enemy.

"Look at their chariots! Those razor-sharp scythes on the wheels! They are machines of death! I have not seen chariots in battle since we made our brief excursion into Britain. I always thought they had their place in wide-open desert warfare, but here in the mountains and valleys, I would not use them."

Caesar focused his attention on Calvinus.

"When the chariots attack, make certain all the infantrymen

have at least two javelins ready. The first line should target the horses and the second line the chariot riders. And repeat with a second volley. The maniples must be ready to wheel and open a space for the chariots and horses that reach our lines. No matter how well they train their horses, the beasts' instincts will overcome their training and they will move toward the open space."

Caesar turned to walk back to his command tent when Calvinus called out, "Sir! The Pontians are coming out of their camp and forming lines."

Caesar sniggered.

"What are they doing?"

Several chariots sped out of the enemy camp, churning up dust in their wake. The charioteers whipped the horses as they steered the war carts in a zigzag course across the open area between the opposing camps. Sunlight flashed brightly from the polished scythes mounted on the wheels. The Pontian infantry began moving down the opposite side of the valley behind the chariots.

Caesar's attention was on the Twenty-Second Legion.

"Good, they are forming up as a precaution. Pharnaces is deploying forces to boost his men's confidence. He knows we will not take up the challenge before we construct our camp. To his men, it will look as if we are afraid. His real intention is to keep part of our men in arms and interfere with the building of our camp."

As more and more of the enemy forces began to mass behind the chariots, Caesar laughed and cried out, "Does he think I am going to fall for this ruse? Pharnaces hopes I will muster the legions and not be able to finish our camp before sundown. And why would he give up such an advantageous position?"

He turned away from the scene and began his tour of the camp and inspection of the perimeter.

#

Aquila worked along with the legionaries of the Sixth as they excavated ditches and pounded stakes to erect the camp's palisades. He heard a commotion in the enemy camp and looked across the valley to the opposite ridge. He watched the infantry of the Twenty-Second halfheartedly form lines three deep, not convinced that Pharnaces's forces intended to attack. *Maniples would be much more effective and could turn and open holes to funnel the chariots.*

The chariots sped in a broad line across the valley floor and started up the slope toward the unfinished Roman camp. Roman bugles sounded to call the legionaries to the lines. Aquila threw down his entrenching tool and grabbed his armor and sword from the stockpile of arms ready near their worksite. As he rushed by the Sixth's standard, he yanked it out of the ground and shouted to his men to call the rest of the Sixth and follow with extra javelins.

A contingent of Roman cavalry charged out to oppose the chariots. They were intercepted by the Pontian cavalry. Calvinus, in charge of the Twenty-Second, had reformed the Roman infantry into maniples, opening holes to funnel the chariots. However, one hundred yards away from the Roman lines and still out of javelin range, the chariots on the outside of the wide line slowed and the formation took the shape of a moving wedge. The wedge quickly grew narrower until the chariots were in single file.

At twenty-five yards, the effective range of a javelin, the lead chariot swung sharply to the left, the second chariot in line turned to the right and the rest of the chariots followed the alternating tactic and swerved with their sides into the infantry line, shredding and mowing down men in the Roman front lines. Limbs, blood, weapons, and debris rained on the legionaries in the second and third lines, spreading terror throughout the ranks. Horses bristled with javelins, ran amok, and dragged chariots over drivers and foot soldiers. However, scores of chariots continued to render their horror as they careened sideways into the lines of Roman infantry, sped away, and then circled back for another run along the battle lines.

Aquila blew his centurion's whistle and waved the Sixth's eagle standard to attract his men to muster around him. As soon as he could form one maniple of 120 men with ranks six deep, he moved them forward and rotated the formation into the path of the racing chariots.

With the chariots bearing down on them at top speed, it took the staunchest discipline for the men to hold their line until Aquila gave the signal to launch their javelins. Three shrill whistles penetrated the din of the battle, and a swarm of over a hundred iron tipped missiles flew toward the chariots. The horses of the lead chariots stumbled and fell, penetrated by the multitude of javelins in the first volley. The drivers and bowmen became casualties as their chariots crashed with the horses, and more were eliminated by the second volley of javelins.

As the rest of the Sixth arrived, the flights of javelins were even more devastating. They picked off one chariot after another. The field became littered with overturned chariots. The remaining chariots slowed as they tried to negotiate the obstacles. They became easy targets as more legionaries arrived from the camp and contributed to the javelins filling the sky. The mayhem from the chariot attack subsided just as the Pontian infantry arrived.

Had they arrived earlier, the Roman lines might have broken during the havoc created by the chariots. The Pontians prevailed in the cavalry skirmish and proceeded to attack the Roman right wing. The veterans of the Sixth let loose a volley of javelins and broke the mounted charge. They were ready to advance, but Pontian heavy infantry pressed into the Twenty-Second and spread the Roman lines thin as they tried to hold the center and left wing. The Roman left wing was pushed back and was almost turned until Caesar brought up the veterans of the Thirty-Sixth Legion, which he had held in reserve. In his haste, he had not brought up his horse, but standing uphill from the enemy he could see his formations well enough. The entry of the Thirty-Sixth into the battle stabilized the lines.

The Roman lines tried to advance. Although the enemy infantry had charged uphill, they still fought fiercely and did not give any ground. Caesar moved near the front lines to rally his men. He was carried by the mass of men, as the Roman left wing pivoted backwards. The Sixth Legion had folded the enemy's left flank back into the rest of their ranks. The crush of men and horses caused such confusion that the Pontian army took flight. The Twenty-Second and Thirty-Sixth legions, relieved of their opposition, paused as they watched the Sixth, less than a thousand strong, chase the scattered remains of the Pontian army.

Caesar had won many battles in his career, many of which were more significant in their outcome. But now he was jubilant that this campaign had come to such a rapid and decisive end. He sent a short message of just three words to the Roman Senate: "Veni, Vidi, Vici"—"I came, I saw, I conquered."

The Roman legionaries were given permission to plunder the enemy camp, but not the city, as Zela was an ally of Rome. The city had suffered much under Pharnaces's occupation. Pharnaces escaped to the coast and set sail to his holdings on the north coast of the Black Sea. Caesar, always a man of quick decisions and haste, was satisfied the region was secure. He departed with a contingent of cavalry to return to Rome and ordered the Sixth to follow him to Italy. There Caesar planned to honor his promise to the Sixth, which after the battle of Zela, had picked up the nickname Legio Ferrata ("The Ironclads"). He would reward them with early retirement and land in southern Gaul.

Aquila searched for Miriam in Zela, but did not find her or her father. Their house had been ransacked by Pharnaces's troops. He left the city on the road to return to the camp, but was hindered by crowds of refugees returning to the city.

Aquila was relieved when he sighted Miriam ahead with a group of men, trudging up the road toward the city gate. They appeared bedraggled and weary. Miriam's dark hair, usually tucked neatly into her headpiece, hung loose and was gray with road dust. She stopped to speak to Aquila and signaled her companions to wait for her.

"Miriam, I'm so relieved you are safe!" He hugged her, but she did not share his enthusiasm and was limp in his embrace. "We checked your house. It was destroyed. How did you survive?"

"We left the city and took refuge in nearby caves that we had prepared for emergencies, but Father refused to leave with us. He was convinced Pharnaces's men were countrymen and would treat us fairly. He was wrong and they killed him. We have just returned from burying him."

"Miriam, I share your sadness and grief. I am so very sorry. I know you must feel a deep emptiness. He was a good man and loved you deeply." He thought he noticed her relax. "Come with me to Italy. I love you, Miriam. It will no longer be safe here."

He stared at her abdomen for a few seconds and then studied her face. Miriam, however, did not show any reaction.

"No, Father would want me to rebuild the business. Besides, I have a large and protective family," she added, as she tilted her head toward the band of men waiting for her. "We will now be secure. Coming back to the city, we passed by your camp and talked with a Roman officer named Caelius Vincianus. He told us the Twenty-Second Legion, made up of Pontians loyal to Rome, will be protecting the province. We will be safe."

"Trusting your countrymen, that was the mistake your father made."

She remained stoic. *She is determined to stay. At least I know she is strong and will raise our child properly. But, no! She must go with me!*

"Miriam, your father told me. You are carrying our child. Don't you want the child to have a father?"

"My child will be raised by our whole family. Father only said that because he wanted you to be my husband."

Aquila explored her eyes. *I cannot tell if she is lying. But I can tell we are over.*

Defeated, Aquila said, "I know Caelius Vincianus. He is a fair and just man and the men of the Twenty-Second are not a bad lot, but you never know. Wait…"

He removed his garnet ring and gave it to her.

"Wear this. The men of the Twenty-Second claim I am their countryman from Pontus. When they see this green ring, they will not allow any mistreatment to befall you or your family."

Aquila slipped the ring on her finger. Miriam's expression softened. As she looked into Aquila's eyes, she choked on her words.

"I cannot leave Zela."

8 TRIBUNE OF THE PLEBEIANS

Seven hundred and eight years after the founding of Rome, spring was showing itself as the trees and flowers began to bud. Aquila rode at a leisurely pace, accompanied by Gnaeus, as they traveled south on the Via Appia to the village of Trebula. Lining the well-traveled road were the tall and narrow pines that dotted the Italian countryside. The trees were uniformly spaced along this stretch of the road. Set back from the pines were thousands of stone tombs and statues of patrician, equestrian, and wealthy plebeians.

"Gnaeus, just a few months ago, I was sweating in armor fighting battles in Pontus. Now I am heading for the comfort of a lavish villa in Samnium. I was intrigued when Cicero said the villa belonged to his friend, Pontius Gaius. And thank you again for your support in my campaign for tribune."

"It's my pleasure, friend, and as Caesar would say, comrade in arms. So, you are now an ex-legionary and will run for office. You have the ideal personality to be a tribune of the plebeians, a sort of magnetism, without the greed for power I see in most politicians. The people will trust you, just as the men did when you were an officer in the legions."

"I owe much to Cicero. Years ago, he trained me to be an advocate and introduced me to many of his political friends in Rome. We'll see him at the Trebula Villa in several days. And I am eager to meet Pontius Gaius."

As they rode on, Aquila remembered his encounter in Rome with Pontius Arenus, a wine merchant introduced to him by Cicero. Arenus had invited him to join them at the Pontius family's evening meal. *Arenus said there were two ancient branches of the Pontius clan. One branch was from the mountains, whose members held sacred the red garnet, the light of the hearth fire. The other branch was from the sea and had been guided in their journey to Italy by the light of their family gem, the green garnet. Separated for generations, the members of the clans eventually made contact. As a memento to this reunion, they crafted identical rings. Each ring was fitted with a red and green garnet. Arenus wore one of the rings and told me he believed the other ring was probably in Samnium, but he had not known who possessed it.*

I could not tell him I gave my ring to Miriam. Instead, I told him my father still possessed a ring with a single green garnet. Arenus was puzzled until I explained the legend Father had told me of the two brothers, one who stayed in Sicily and one who traveled to Italy. Arenus found the variation to the legend fascinating and was convinced there must be a connection. He believes we are distantly related.

He wholeheartedly pledged his support for my election to plebeians' tribune. He said he knew many people in Rome and promised he would collect their votes for his "cousin." And finally, I wrote to Father in Sicily. He will be fascinated to hear about the other Pontii legend.

Gnaeus interrupted Aquila's thoughts as he said, "Cicero is

like a father to you. What about your family in Sicily? You do not talk much of them."

Aquila looked over at his friend.

"Are you prescient? I was just thinking about them. I will go back soon, now that the civil war is over."

Gnaeus added, "When you return to Rome, you must invite me to your new house. How did you manage to buy it? Were the spoils of war that profitable?"

"Remember Juventius? He moved to southern Gaul and took claim to his portion of the land Caesar awarded to retirees from the Sixth. He sold my allotment and I used the cash to purchase a small house." Aquila added with a chuckle, "Can you imagine Juventius becoming a farmer?"

"Aquila, I see Caesar kept his word this time. I had heard that he promises land and spoils to his legions, but when it comes time, he instead persuades them to fight one more battle."

"That is all true. The Sixth fought in Egypt, and then after the losses at Zela, the legion had barely two cohorts left, less than a thousand men. It was easier for Caesar to reward this smaller force as it would not deplete his army significantly. And the payment—the lands he awarded—was not great compared to what he would have had to award if he had allowed the Tenth and the Ninth to retire, as he had promised."

"What happened to you, Aquila? I assumed you were loyal to Caesar. What soldier cannot love him? Even his enemies cannot hold back their admiration! His clemency for those he defeats is famous!"

"I am torn between Caesar and the Republic. I am compelled to support him. He can capture your spirit with a

156

word. When the Tenth intended to revolt, he pacified them by agreeing to their demands for retirement and wealth. When he made his farewell speech, he addressed them as citizens rather than comrades in arms. Insulted and feeling alienated, the legionaries pleaded with him to take them back, agreeing to fight for him in Spain. With one word, he had turned them around."

"Aquila, he has conquered new and valuable lands for Rome. He has shown great clemency with his enemies, unlike Sulla who sentenced death to anyone who supported his opponents. As long as Caesar lives, Rome and Romans will prosper."

"But what will happen after he is gone? If he destroys our republican institutions, there will be nothing left to stop the next powerful man and another civil war. It is better for the people to retain what freedom they have with the Republic."

The men rode in silence, Aquila evaluating the pros and cons of the argument.

"Gnaeus, I was loyal to my men, to my friends, to you. Yes, I loved and was sometimes blindly loyal to Caesar, particularly when he was my superior officer. But in the last few years I have seen that he has turned more greedy and ambitious. He is not for Rome or the Republic. He is even reported to have said that the Republic is just an image, not a reality! He is for himself. Yes, he has won many battles due to his keen tactical skills and leadership, but he has had some luck, too. He boasted about Zela because it ended so quickly. But it was the ineptness of Pharnaces and the mettle of Caesar's men that won the battle. He would show real greatness if he returned to Rome as a humble servant of the Roman people, like Cincinnatus, like Scipio, yes, like even the late Pompeius."

"Be careful, Aquila. Do not test the extent of Caesar's

clemency. There are many who would inform Caesar. I am certain that in public you will be more tactful."

Aquila continued, as if he did not hear Gnaeus's warning.

"I'll tell you this, Caesar is a genius. He is the master manipulator. Sure, there are those who follow just because they think he will be the winner. But he appears strong and virtuous to the common people. He does enough to put on a show, like retiring the Sixth, to make everyone think they will get their reward, too. But it is mere politics! You were there in the Forum at the Rostra during the Lupercalian Festival when Antonius Marcus offered Caesar the crown of a king. He rejected it, but I have heard the whole affair was contrived to crush the rumors that Caesar would consider being a king. Why bother with such a display? What is the difference if he is now Dictator . . . not one appointed by law during a national emergency, but . . . for life? He is the sole consul this year, because no one was brave enough to govern with him.

"I agree with what he once said. He probably does not even remember what he said: 'People will believe what they want to believe. And many go so far as to think everyone else should also believe what they believe.'"

Gnaeus tried to change the subject, and looking ahead as they rode said, "Calm yourself, Aquila, you are just working yourself into a frenzy. The Republic will endure as it always has, just as when Sulla gave up the dictatorship. Besides, we can soon relax at the villa. I am looking forward to some cool wine, when . . ."

Gnaeus looked over at his friend, but Aquila was not listening. Aquila's jaw muscles were clenched, his face drawn tight, and tears of anger coursed down his cheeks.

Within several hours, they arrived at the Trebula Villa and were surprised that Cicero had preceded them and had organized a welcome party. He had invited notable Romans of all classes. It was a wonder that so many had come to the small village, but Cicero had arranged for guests to stay in the numerous rooms of the sprawling villa as well as several friends' villas, including one of his own. The large and prosperous Greco-Roman city of Capua was only an hour's ride, and Trebula was only a short fifteen-minute ride off the Via Appia. The largest Samnium city in the area, Beneventum, was two hours away by horse or carriage.

Aquila spent the afternoon and evening being introduced to many influential and wealthy friends and associates of Cicero. It took all his stamina to keep up his appearance and present an optimistic and energetic front. He made up for his limited knowledge of Roman legal matters and politics by telling entertaining stories of the foreign lands he had served and campaigned in.

Eventually, Aquila walked outside to be alone beside the pool, but Cicero called out from behind him, "Lucius, you will definitely want to see..."

Aquila was tired. His mind screamed.

No more introductions!

Before Aquila turned, a vision flashed through his mind of Tullia, remembering her on the Sicilian beach. His premonition became reality as he turned and saw her, more mature, her vivaciousness projected in her brilliant smile. As he gazed into her sparkling green eyes, the fatigue and weariness fell away and new energy filled him.

The next day, Aquila woke to bright sunshine. He had slept

until afternoon. He made his way outside to a large marble terrace that faced west toward the sea. In the distance, he saw a blue-and-white haze where the sea transitioned to sky. A pleasant coolness lingered as the sun cast warmth on the veranda. The quietude convinced him the guests had departed. Tullia, Gnaeus, Cicero, and an unfamiliar man were enjoying a modest meal seated at a round marble table, rather than reclining on the couches common for the longer meals. As Aquila approached the group, the stranger noticed and smiled. Cicero introduced them.

"Aquila, I hope you slept well. Meet my friend Pontius Gaius. He was most gracious to let us use his country villa for our election symposium. Gaius spends most of his time in his home in Beneventum."

Gaius nodded his head to greet Aquila. A sparkle caught Aquila's eye and he glanced at the man's left hand, noticing a gold ring imbedded with two gems, one red and one green. Since his father had given him the green garnet ring, Aquila had developed a habit of flicking his left thumb against his ring finger as if to satisfy himself the ring was still there. The sight of Gaius's ring triggered the habit and he was reminded that he no longer possessed the ring.

"Gaius, I have only passed through your city on the Via Appia. Tell me about it. Do you enjoy living there?"

"Our family lives in the countryside near the city. We raise goats and cattle to produce cheese and leather goods, which we sell in Beneventum and Capua. I do take pleasure living in the country. I am intrigued that we have the same surname, but I am also interested in the origin of the name Aquila. Were you given the name while you served in the legions?"

"Yes. I was with Caesar in Gaul. During the Battle of

Gergovia, the Aquila of the Sixth Legion was lost. I recovered the standard and my comrades began calling me Aquila. It stuck."

"What a remarkable deed! I am certain you earned such an honorable name. My father also acquired a cognomen as a legionary. He was among the first Samnites to serve in the Roman legions. Most Samnites are very skilled in the use of the pilum. However, his accuracy was exceptional, so the centurions called him Pilatus. He went on to train the new recruits in the use of the weapon."

"Gaius, speaking of the family name, Pontius Arenus, whom I met in Rome, said the Pontii are descended from two branches. One group, comprised of mountain folk, is represented by the red garnet. The Pontii of the other branch were associated with the sea, and are represented by the green garnet. Arenus wore a ring identical to yours."

"Yes, I know of that legend. I can tell you that the Samnites are the mountain clan. As for association with the sea, the Roman Pontii may be able to tell you more. Wouldn't it be amazing if they are ancestors of the Trojans who sailed to Italy with Aeneas? This is fascinating! I hope we can talk more of family history another time. But, today, I understand there may be some way I can help you."

"Yes, sir. I am seeking election as Tribune of the Plebeians and ask for your support, Gaius."

"That will not be difficult. Not only do I believe we are distant kin, but we will support anyone who is recommended by Cicero. I will spread the word in Beneventum to support you, Cousin. In fact, I will begin today, as I must return to take care of some business in the city. Good luck on your campaign." He stood and said his farewells. Cicero escorted him to the stables to see him off.

Gnaeus, exhausted from the ride from Rome and the symposium the previous night, excused himself for an afternoon nap. Cicero retired to a quiet room in the villa to write. Tullia and Aquila reminisced and strolled for hours about the landscaped grounds. The sun set into the Tyrrhenian Sea.

"I'm so pleased you came with your father. This campaigning is tiresome. But what a pleasant surprise, here we are, enjoying this beautiful full moon."

Tullia wrapped herself in her cloak as the night air rapidly cooled. Aquila put his arm around her shoulders as they nestled together.

"I am so content and I feel cared for when I am with you. The only other time I feel this way is with Father."

"So, I am a father figure to you!"

"No, no, I don't mean it that way. I don't think of you as my father, you know that."

Aquila chuckled.

"Of course, I am so proud of Father. I feel his love, even when he is far away. Despite the problems I have had in my marriages, he still supports me. When my first child died and Dolabella was so distant, Father made great efforts to keep a relationship with him for my welfare."

"I owe your father much, but he never makes me feel obligated. He is like a father to me too. But it was hard for me to leave the legions. I admire and think of my former comrades often. When I fought for Rome, it was for the Republic. Now with Cicero's help, I am compelled to seek election."

As the moon climbed in the clear sky overhead, they found

a private spot in the garden. Aquila spread his cloak on the ground. They lay together and covered themselves with Tullia's cloak to ward off the chill, and consummated a perfect evening.

#

After the morning meal, Aquila said farewells to Tullia, Gnaeus, and Cicero. Gnaeus mounted his horse with the help of a stable hand.

Aquila called out, "Are you a cavalry officer or what? I would expect you to vault onto your horse, soldier!"

Gnaeus had a broad smile as he guffawed. "Ha! Aquila, I am glad to see you are feeling better today!"

As Tullia and Cicero sat in the coach readying for their return north to Rome, Cicero leaned out of the window.

"Aquila, you are the brave one now. Lately, whenever I have seen a threat, I have either exiled myself voluntarily or allowed myself to be exiled until the conflict settled. You are flying right into the jaws of danger. I used to do that when I was younger. Now the student has set the example for the teacher. Remember, the true way, the right way, is to serve the people."

Cicero reached out to Aquila and gently pulled him closer. He whispered, "The truth is still the best way, even though your enemies can predict your actions. There will be a time in your life when you may have to exploit that trust and do something against all you stand for. But always take that advantage only if it is for the good. Save that time for a great decision."

Cicero sat back.

"I will see you in Rome soon."

#

The next year passed rapidly as Aquila campaigned in and around Rome. Then in the late summer of C. Julius Caesar IV COS, his hard work came to fruition, and Aquila easily won his election as tribune of the plebeians, a representative of the common people. The first months of Tribune Pontius Aquila's service were not much different than the routine of a wealthy patrician or equestrian. He received clients each morning and spent the hot afternoons at the baths in discussions with the influential men of Rome. Twice he had used the tribune's veto to block the passage of laws which would have harmed the plebeians' rights.

By late fall, Aquila's political career continued to be a success. Dolabella, however, who switched political sides at a whim and lacked any moral restraints, divorced Tullia. Aquila had not seen her since Trebula, and he went to comfort her after he heard about her divorce. During his visit, he discovered she was pregnant. He was relieved that she was optimistic and eager to have a healthy child.

Caesar defeated Pompeius's supporters in North Africa and Spain where he won the final military campaign of the civil war. He had left Antonius Marcus in Rome to enforce his dictatorship, but Marcus seemed to be more interested in elegant parties than Senate meetings. There was growing excitement among the populace when Caesar returned to Rome. The people anticipated the parades and exhibits he would hold, the Triumphs to celebrate his victories in battles in Asia and in Egypt.

Along the broad street running parallel to the Forum and leading past the Senate building, benches had been placed for senators, magistrates, tribunes, and other dignitaries to observe the Triumph. Their seats were set back from the street on the upper steps of wide concrete flights leading to the Senate building, temples, and other large public buildings. This not only gave the officials an elevated vantage point to observe the spectacle, but they were in turn easily observable by those in the parade.

Crowds of onlookers gathered below and in front of the officials and lined the street. Cicero declined Aquila's offer to sit next to him with the tribunes, explaining it would be more of an honor for Aquila to sit alone with other currently elected officials. In this way, Aquila would appear as a self-made man rather than his protégé. Aquila joined the other nine tribunes on the top row of seats at the Senate house. Cicero assembled with four hundred members of the Senate.

Aquila surveyed the long procession of wagons filled with treasures. Accompanying them were throngs of captured slaves, collections of exotic foreign animals, and legionaries dressed in brilliantly polished armor. It was a sunny but mild day, perfect weather for such an outdoor event. The cheerful and excited voices of the people fashioned a buoyant atmosphere. Snack vendors were everywhere shouting and hawking. The aroma of sausages, cheese, and fresh bread soaked in olive oil wafted through the air.

Several days prior, Caesar had celebrated a massive and splendid Triumph for his numerous battles of the campaign in Gaul. No Roman general had ever held a Triumph for a victory over other Romans, and Caesar did not commemorate the Battle of Pharsalus. The terrible sentiments of countrymen fighting countrymen were still fresh in people's minds.

The first elements of the Triumph appeared as battle horns blared and legionaries of the Tenth Legion marched by, their hobnailed sandals snapping on the pavement. Forty elephants and other exotic animals from Africa followed, representing the Egyptian campaign and celebrating the victory at the Battle of Alexandria. The next contingent, representing the victory at Zela, was led by scores of chariots. Glistening metal scythes fitted on the axles rotated and flashed in the sun and presented a vicious spectacle as the vehicles paraded by. In this Pontic Triumph, Caesar displayed among the showpieces of the procession an inscription of the three words he had sent to the Senate announcing his victory at Zela: "Veni, Vidi, Vici" (I came, I saw, I conquered), indicating the speed with which the campaign had finished. After hours of display, there was a lull in the grand procession and people began leaning into the street searching for Caesar, expecting to see him next, riding in a chariot.

As the Dictator's chariot moved slowly along the street, the Senators and tribunes showed their respect and rose from their seats, standing one after another creating a wave of movement along the procession. Aquila refused to stand as Caesar's chariot passed in front of him. Caesar's eyes locked on Aquila, surrounded by the other tribunes now all on their feet. Caesar shouted, looking back at Aquila as the procession moved on,

"Hey, there, Aquila, the Tribune! Do you want me to restore the Republic?"

Later that evening, Aquila returned home and chose not to make the rounds with his friends at the house and street parties. They were extensions of the parades and spectacles of the day and he could hear the shouts and revelry of citizens laughing and partying in the streets. He sat alone in his house, sipping wine and reading by oil lamp a history of Lucius Brutus, who had led the revolt that disposed of the last king of Rome almost five hundred years earlier.

Aquila heard a knock at the front door, surprising him. His doorman came into the room and announced Cicero had arrived. Aquila met Cicero and his brother Quintus in the peristylium garden, which surrounded a small pool. Both brothers had broad smiles and their eyes were glassy, having had an abundant share of wine at parties throughout the city. Aquila's servant brought pitchers of water and wine as they sat with Aquila. Cicero smiled.

"Aquila, you are missing all the merriment. The citizens are enjoying all the free food, wine, and entertainment that Caesar has supplied. My, how you have changed since you went to war."

Quintus added, "I agree. When we finished a campaign and were given leave, I remember Aquila partook in the amusements and elixir as much as the rest of us."

Aquila raised his cup.

"To Lucius Brutus, who freed us from tyranny; to the Republic!"

Cicero's smile turned to a frown.

"Oh, I see. You are still distraught about Caesar's behavior. I heard about what happened today—the words he had with you. Well, perhaps it is good you are lying low tonight."

Cicero looked earnestly at his brother, who continued as if on cue.

"Aquila, remember several days ago, when two tribunes jailed the citizen who had put the king's crown on the statue of Caesar? When Caesar found out, he stripped the tribunes of their office. It appears that Caesar, in his arrogance, has annulled one of the oldest Roman laws: the immunity of the Tribune of the

Plebs. No one, not even a Consul, has the right to harm or interfere with a Plebs Tribune. Aquila, that's why we are here. We are here to warn you. If Caesar would do this to them, what do you think he has planned for you? The word is that he wants revenge."

Aquila peered at Cicero, at Quintus, and then back at Cicero. Both men sat stone-faced in silence. When Aquila became agitated and was about to curse Caesar, the brothers could not retain their composure. Both burst out laughing.

Aquila could not help but laugh with them, but after the hilarity died down, now unfazed, he said, "A good joke. Yes, yes. Caesar was very irritated by my refusal to stand at the Triumph."

When they both looked at each other and resumed their uncontrolled mirth, Aquila said, "Wait, both of you. Is it the wine doing this? There is something else. What is so funny?"

Quintus answered, "You had to be there, Aquila. You should have heard Caesar. Cicero, you take the role of Caesar." The pair, uninhibited now and loosened by wine, reenacted their comic tale. Quintus picked up his cup and a pitcher of water and addressed Cicero, "O noble Caesar, do you want water with your wine?"

Cicero took his time choosing. "Um, let's see, what do I want? Should I ask Pontius Aquila what will be best?"

That brought a smile and chuckle from Aquila.

"He said that?"

Both nodded in agreement as Quintus held an imaginary scroll out to Cicero.

"Dictator, will you sign this law to increase the grain distribution to the people?"

Cicero rubbed his chin and then said, "Only with Pontius Aquila's permission!"

Aquila chuckled heartily. His mirth increased with each new rendition the brothers enacted, as they quoted Caesar. "If Pontius Aquila will allow it." The fact that Caesar was so obsessed with Aquila's renunciation at the Triumph further fueled their hilarity. After their laughter died down and they wiped the tears from their eyes, Cicero added, "Lucius, uh... Aquila, you got the best of Caesar today. When we heard him answer like that several times tonight, we had to refrain from laughter, and finally had to walk outside. According to others we talked to, Caesar apparently relived his exasperation for most of the day and well into the night."

\#

Over the next months, Caesar's behavior became more and more arrogant and even the common people who had idolized him felt Caesar was ignoring and destroying Roman traditions. Graffiti of sarcastic poems and demeaning slogans appeared on many statues of Caesar around Rome.

At first, small independent factions of senators conspired to find ways to limit Caesar's power. These groups eventually gravitated to one another, forming a conspiracy of over sixty senators, equestrians, and like-minded citizens. The collection of conspirators became known as the Liberatores.

Aquila agreed to join, with the strict stipulation that Cicero would not be recruited and would not know of the plans. Aquila believed that if the plot failed, the only hope for any future reemergence of the Republic was with Cicero's survival and leadership. Moreover, Aquila felt the activity sullied Cicero's morals and ethics.

Others had their priorities, such as one of the Liberatores's leaders, Decimus Junius Brutus, the governor of Cisalpine Gaul. He insisted that Antonius Marcus and Lepidus, Caesar's closest allies, be spared, since the elimination of Caesar should not be considered a rebellion. Their objectives were to free the Republic and for it to function properly, not to take control of the government.

On March 15, the Ides of March, C. Julius Caesar V and Antonius Marcus COS, Aquila sat in his usual place at the Senate meeting. He was a tribune and not a senator, so he sat in the back in the upper levels, far from the front and center of power where the most senior and powerful senators assembled. He had agreed to participate in the assassination of Caesar, but from his vantage point it would be hard to get through over four hundred senators to take part in the execution. Thus, his role was to impede senators that might assist Caesar or resist the Liberatores.

As far as Aquila observed, it was proceeding as planned. The date was set to precede Caesar's planned invasion of Parthia in the East, since that would mean his absence from Rome for several years. To the conspirators' advantage, weeks earlier, Caesar had discontinued having his Spanish bodyguards accompany him in public.

As the Senate had assembled, Liberatores had distracted and delayed Antonius Marcus outside in the Forum. Senator Casca approached Caesar carrying a scroll describing a proposed law for his review. When Caesar dismissed him with a wave of his hand, a group of the Liberatores crowded around the dictator. Casca grabbed the collar of Caesar's toga and drew a dagger. His thrust only glanced off Caesar's neck.

Caesar appeared upset but was unaware as to the extent of the threat. Thinking this was an isolated attack, he shouted, "What is this violence?"

The other assassins hesitated, but then all began pushing ahead, each stabbing him in turn as Caesar fell to the floor. Mayhem and shouting filled the hall as conspirators and innocents alike rushed out into the streets.

The hall had almost emptied as Aquila, dagger in his hand, approached Caesar's bloodied body on the floor. He looked down at the lifeless form as he recalled that the Liberatores had made an agreement that all were to share the undertaking. Each would pierce the dictator to share the responsibility. However, he had no intention now in adding to the wounds.

Cicero was hurrying out the door, then stopped and said, "You knew! You were part of this! Leave now! There will be mobs in the streets. Let them vent their anger. Tomorrow will be a new day, a day when the Republic is reborn." Cicero took several steps, stopped, and looked back again. "Aquila, congratulations on a job well done!" He rushed out, distancing himself from the tragedy.

#

As Aquila hurried to his house, the sense of uncertainty recurred that had plagued him since the conspiracy had been planned. *What would have happened if the assassination had not occurred? Caesar always held Alexander the Great in high esteem. Even with all that Caesar accomplished in his fifty years of life, rumors spread that he wept when he visited Alexander's tomb in Egypt, understanding that Alexander had already conquered the world when he was just thirty years old. The*

171

effects of Alexander's accomplishments, even in his short lifetime, established Greek culture over large areas of the East and have endured for hundreds of years after his death.

Had Caesar lived, I am certain that he would have avenged Crassus's defeat and conquered the Parthians. And knowing Caesar, he would not have stopped. The lasting effects of Caesar's works would have endured for thousands of years. The future for Rome would truly have been unending glory.

The Senate, desiring to avoid further violence, convened the next day and granted amnesty to all the assassins. Antonius Marcus, expecting to be named Caesar's successor and beneficiary of Caesar's fortune, gave a public speech praising his friend and gaining the support of the plebeians.

Caesar's will was read in public. To Marcus's dismay, Caesar's grandnephew, his adopted son Octavius, was designated as his heir, not Marcus. Caesar had left a small amount of cash to every citizen in the city of Rome. The common people revered Caesar and demanded that he be cremated in the Forum. Several public buildings were set on fire in the ensuing riots. Innocent men, mistakenly accused as being Caesar's assassins, were killed by the mobs. Although the riots subsided over the next weeks, the feeling that the amnesty would not last much longer compelled most of the Liberatores to leave the city.

Loyalties and alliances among Republicans, Caesar's assassins, and former Caesar supporters became blurred in the days following the assassination. Decimus Brutus returned to Cisalpine Gaul, where he continued as governor with several legions stationed there still loyal to him. The Senate, perceiving this as a threat to their power, ordered Brutus to immediately give up command of the legions and return to Rome. Emergency elections were held. Two new consuls, Pansa Catronianius and Aulus Hirtius, were elected to lead the senatorial legions.

Antonius Marcus, with the support of Caesar's former legions, began parleying with the Senate to share power. The Senate shrewdly directed Marcus to Gaul to remove Decimus Brutus as well as to decrease the threat of Marcus's legions stationed near Rome. He took up the challenge, perceiving it as a way to increase his influence. Once Marcus was on his way north, Cicero gave a rousing speech to the Senate, vilifying Marcus as a continuation of Caesar's dictatorship. The Senate declared Marcus an enemy of the state.

Brutus fled to Mutina, a fortified town south of the Po River in Cisalpine Gaul. Knowing of Aquila's staunch support of the Republic and his experience as an officer in the legions, Brutus sent for Aquila to join him.

In Rome, Aquila hurriedly packed his equipment and prepared to join Brutus. *The clemency granted to Caesar's assassins will not last long. Brutus doesn't trust the Senate. Neither should I. But if I join Brutus, there is a chance we may restore the Republic.*

Aquila's doorman informed him a slave had brought a message from Cicero, requesting Aquila see him before he left Rome. The city was in turmoil. The streets were clogged with carts and litters carrying nobles and senators fleeing Rome. Aquila made his way through the crowds to Cicero's house. The noise and mayhem continued inside the house as slaves rushed to pack family belongings.

Cicero heartily embraced Aquila. He whispered, "There are eyes and ears in the walls. My diatribe denouncing Antonius Marcus placed my family in grave danger. I am remaining in Rome, but I am sending everyone in my household away to a safe location."

Cicero released Aquila from his hold and became unsteady. He convulsed and wept. "My beautiful Tullia never recovered from her son's birth several weeks ago. I lost her last night! My Tulliola is dead!"

Aquila collapsed into a chair and covered his face with his hands. "No!"

Cicero calmed and said, "We have prepared her ashes for burial in the Tullii plot on the Via Appia. When this crisis is over, you and I will go together and visit her grave."

A dark-haired young woman entered the room cradling a baby. Looking through his tears, Aquila barely recognized Prisca, Tullia's lifelong friend.

Cicero gently placed his hand on Aquila's shoulder.

"Aquila, when I heard you were leaving Rome I knew I had to inform you that before my Tullia . . . our . . . Tullia died, she told me this beautiful boy is your son."

Aquila was stunned. So much had happened over the last few days. He was physically and emotionally drained. There were so many unexpected shocks and so much pressure. He barely heard Cicero's next words.

"Prisca will care for the child as if he was her own. I have taken the liberty to rewrite your will, leaving your estate to her and the boy. Now, for their safety, they will evacuate along with the household."

Aquila stood frozen and speechless. He could not make a decision.

"Son, in these unstable times, you can trust very few people. Anyone who is not family should be suspect. Everyone is maneuvering to support who they think will triumph. Octavius knows you were a Liberatore. Antonius Marcus wants my head, and he still retains the loyalty of many powerful people in Rome. Yet I feel my duty is in Rome to maintain some stability. Moreover, if I were to flee with my family, my presence would put them in mortal danger."

"Cicero, you have had more time to plan. I have just discovered now that I have a son. I am desperate as to the best decision for me—for us. I do not trust Brutus, yet I have no other choice. It is the only hope for my son to live in a republic, where citizens have freedom."

Prisca handed the baby to Aquila. "Here is your son, Aquila. Tullia named him Marianus, after your father."

As Aquila kissed the boy on the forehead, his eyes met Prisca's. For an instant, he imagined she was Tullia but shook his head to rid himself of the delusion. He handed Marianus back to her.

"Yes, I will fight for my son! I will fight for Marianus!"

Aquila staggered out of the house. Cicero shouted after him, "Son, remember this. Remember where you met Pontius Gaius!"

Aquila rushed through the streets and across the Tiber to the stables. His servant had readied his armor and military kit. He galloped north on his Sicilian mount.

9 MUTINA

When Aquila arrived in Mutina, Decimus Brutus promoted him to second in command. Aquila circulated among Brutus's troops and found that the legionaries were mostly Romanized Gauls and Ligurians. They had been promised citizenship if they served for at least ten years in the legions. Facing them would be Italian legions who had served under Caesar and who had passed their loyalty over to Antonius Marcus. Aquila became acquainted with as many soldiers as possible and then prepared a motivating speech. He emphasized that they were fighting on home soil, for their freedom and to preserve their right to send tribunes to Rome as their representatives. Failure would mean reinstating the ancient rights of the wealthy patrician families to be the sole members of the Senate.

Brutus moved supplies into Mutina to prepare the fortified city as a base against the legions led by Antonius Marcus, now moving up from the southeast along the Via Aemilia. Marcus's ally, T. Munatius Plancus, approached from the west with a large contingent of cavalry. Marcus's plan was to attack Brutus's legions from two directions.

Brutus wanted Aquila to intercept Plancus.

"Aquila, you must cripple and destroy Plancus's force. We need time to improve the fortifications of Mutina. After you defeat Plancus you must immediately return to Mutina. It will be very difficult to hold out if we must face both forces at once, and we will need every man. Plancus rides with at least two thousand. You will take all of our cavalry."

"Sir, you will need to retain some cavalry scouts and skirmishers here. Without them, you will be blind to Marcus's approach. I advise you keep one cavalry cohort. Many of the Gallic soldiers you have trained as infantry grew up riding horses. They may not know cavalry tactics, but by adding mounted infantry to my troops it will allow me more options to engage Plancus. I recommend that I take three of the four cavalry cohorts along with three mounted infantry cohorts."

Brutus studied Aquila, hesitated, and then answered, "Very well, but make certain you return before Marcus arrives."

Aquila immediately sent several riders west to find the location of Plancus's force. Within an hour, Aquila had his men prepared and they moved northwest along the Via Amelia. Forty miles south of Mediolanum they turned west on the Via Domitia, which led to Narbonese Gaul and eventually into Spain.

#

In Rome, the Senate scrambled to organize troops in the event Antonius Marcus defeated Brutus and returned demanding concessions. Octavius took command of the elite Praetorian Cohort stationed in Rome. Cicero addressed the Senate and the citizens in the Forum. He was determined to show them the way back to their ancient republican traditions. The citizens of Rome seemed eager to listen to the famous orator as Cicero spoke.

"Romans, Octavius stands here as one of you, as a Roman

citizen, returned from his former military service and now ready again to serve Rome in the spirit of Cincinnatus. And just as his great uncle, Caesar, issued clemency, Octavius has forgiven Caesar's assassins. Octavius is now ready to fight alongside former enemies against Antonius Marcus's obsession to be dictator, the real threat to Romans' freedoms and rights. Octavius will not make the same mistakes that Caesar made, but true to our traditions, will heed the advice from the wisdom of the Senate and the people of Rome, the Senatus Populus Que Romanus."

After Cicero's speech, Octavius, only nineteen years old but an intelligent, serious, and well-educated young man, sought out Cicero.

"Sir, I am regretful that your vision for Rome and Caesar's dream were not in more harmony. I know he wanted you as a close associate in his plans and had deep respect for you. Had you joined him, you might have influenced him to temper himself. Perhaps the tragedy would not have befallen him and he would still be alive."

Cicero was silent for several moments as he evaluated Octavius. He fell back on his intuition, which in years of experience had served him well in detecting the moral status of an individual. He looked into Octavius's eyes and decided Octavius was sincere.

"Son, we cannot change what has happened but can only learn from it and not repeat the same mistakes. Because of the way Marcus recently addressed the Senate, I am afraid he has visions of being king of Rome. Make certain he does not return to Rome as a conqueror, but as a citizen ready to serve Rome."

The next day, Hurtius, one of the newly elected consuls, mobilized the sole legion garrisoned near Rome and united his troops with Octavius and the Praetorian Cohort. The combined force marched north on the Via Aemilia. The second consul, Pansa, planned to follow as soon as two additional legions stationed in southern Italy arrived in Rome.

#

Marcus Vincentus Decius was skilled at bringing out the best in a horse, and he loved a race. Decius urged his mount to gallop ahead of his scouting partner, Manlius, who was not far behind. The horses made fast time, speeding west along the Via Domitia through the valley of the Tanarus River as they hunted for Plancus and his cavalry. He did not slow any as he rode rapidly through the village of Pollentia, situated along the north bank of the river. The sound of his mount's hooves reverberated loudly between the stone buildings and echoed across the fields surrounding the hamlet. Known for its production of brown wool and pottery, the small town was busy with the traffic of the trades. People scrambled out of the way as he sped down the street. After swiftly clearing the village, he was aware that his partner was not far behind. He could hear the sounds of Manlius's steed on the pavement, resonating behind him.

The pair rode over an hour and did not encounter Plancus's troops. Decius slowed his mount to a stop as his partner caught up. The horses breathed heavily with exhaustion.

"Manlius, Aquila ordered us to find a strategic location. Return and tell Aquila to plan an ambush at Pollentia, the last village we passed. I will go on and find Plancus."

When Aquila arrived in Pollentia, he placed the infantry on the roofs of the buildings which lined the Via Domitia as it wound through the village. He hid his cavalry on the east side of the town. The Tanarus River flanked the south side of the town.

Just as he mounted his horse to survey the troop positions, Aquila heard a shout from the west. He scanned the flat fields and saw his scout, Decius, furiously urging his horse as it galloped ahead of two enemy scouts in close pursuit. Aquila sent a handful of mounted troops to Decius's defense. The enemy scouts reined in their mounts and turned back the direction they had come.

Aquila organized a cohort of cavalry and led them west along the Via Domitia. Within minutes they met the vanguard of Plancus's cavalry. He recognized the legate and led a charge into their ranks. Plancus spread his forces to outflank Aquila's troops. Aquila executed the planned retreat and fled down the road into Pollentia with the enemy cavalry in pursuit.

A hail of javelins from the infantry on rooftops and those blocking the street tore into Plancus's troops. At the same time, Aquila's cavalry reserves that had circled the village charged into the flanks of Plancus's cavalry still coming down the Via Domitia.

Routed in less than half an hour, Plancus escaped with only several hundred of his men by crossing the river and fleeing west. With Plancus's force now ineffective, and with just an hour of daylight remaining, Aquila urged his men toward Mutina. During the ride, the adrenaline and the rush of battle drained from him.

What was I doing charging ahead of my men? It was unnecessary at the time. Not only that, but I have ordered the troops to travel in the dark for several hours. We will have to sleep tonight without the security of a fortified camp. Have I already forgotten that I have a son? Caesar would have surveyed from a distance, kept his reserves ready until the critical moment, and only entered the battle himself when it was necessary. I was reckless. Why am I using Caesar's strategies as a guide? It is better for Rome that he is dead. But . . . is it? This civil war would not be happening if Caesar was still alive. I did the wrong thing, joining the Liberatores. But it's too late now. He regained control. *All that counts now is my son! I will fight, and I will survive!*

At first light, Aquila's forces broke camp and rushed eastward. Within several hours, they approached the city of Mutina. The chief scout Decius pulled up and reported, forcing out his words as he tried to recover his breath.

"Legate, two cohorts of cavalry from Antonius Marcus's legions are only a half a mile away, approaching at a trot from the south on the Via Aemilia. A legion of infantry is several miles behind, moving at standard marching speed. Two of his legions are constructing fortified camps on the other side of the river. Decimus Brutus has decided to remain in the city."

"Who is leading the cavalry?"

"It is Antonius Marcus himself."

Aquila turned to the tribune who was his second in command.

"Direct the mounted infantry to the city and stage the third cavalry cohort in reserve near the north city gate."

The tribune split off with his assigned legionaries and proceeded to Mutina. Aquila sent several scouts along the Via Aemilia to check Marcus's position. He then followed with two cavalry cohorts.

As they rode, Aquila knew he was taking a risk. If Marcus's infantry caught up before he engaged the enemy cavalry, he would be vastly outnumbered. Aquila recalled the news he had heard from Rome. *Cicero blasted Antonius Marcus with speech after speech, accusing him of wanting to become heir to Caesar's dictatorship. The Senate was convinced and declared Antonius Marcus an enemy of the Republic. Cicero was right, of course, but he put himself in a dangerous position.*

Aquila passed through seeded fields yet to show growth and Marcus's force came into view. In the distance were the northern ridges of the Apennine Mountains, dark with forests of pines.

Centurions shouted commands and both forces began to spread out in battle lines. Reserves were positioned in the rear. Marcus led his own right wing. Aquila respected the man for his courage although he loathed him for his lack of principles.

When the two forces came within a hundred paces of each other, both slowed and stopped advancing. Marcus rode out from his men into the open space and shouted,

"Aquila! Lucius Pontius Aquila! Tribune of the Plebeians, come and talk to me, old friend."

Antonius Marcus's armor was of the highest quality and the sunlight flashed off the brilliant surface. The blood-red horsehair crest on the top of his helmet matched his cape, the color he had adopted from Caesar. Marcus was considered a handsome man and had profound concern about his appearance. The black Sicilian stallion he rode complemented him well.

Aquila could see that Marcus's face was immaculate and cleanly shaven. The smile on his face did not fool Aquila. He remembered from experience that the expression on the man's face never matched his intent.

Behind both commanders, the legionaries held their lines almost motionless, with only the occasional chink of armor or weapons and the sporadic snort of a horse. Aquila and Marcus both moved ahead to the midpoint between the formations of troops.

"Aquila! Caesar was like a father to me . . . and also to you, brother. So, I cannot understand why you were against him. Caesar knew Rome was too big to be a republic, and has been for a long time. Join us, and carry on his vision."

Aquila felt the wildness rising within him. His first urge was to cry out that he agreed with Marcus, but he held himself in check and remained silent.

Marcus's smile did not change as he said, "We should unite. I would be happy to welcome a true soldier to our ranks. Some of these men were with you at Gergovia and they saw you save the eagle."

"What do you really want?" Aquila asked.

"How about your two cohorts versus mine? I will not use my infantry. What glory it will be! We'll see who has trained the best cavalry, the teacher or the student." Marcus's horse became restless and had to be restrained, as if the creature sensed the challenge to fight.

Aquila realized, as Marcus's persuasive efforts became decidedly foolish, that this whole exchange was a ploy for Marcus's infantry to close the distance. He answered, "This is not about you. Rome is not about one man. Rome is about the people, the Roman people now and those five hundred years ago who fought to establish a republic."

Marcus exploded in laughter. Aquila reined in his mount to return to his men. Marcus's horse rose up on its hind legs, its fore hooves flailing the air threatening to come down on

Aquila's back. Aquila purposely ignored the threat, though his horse pitched forward at the last instant, away from the impending danger. As Aquila deliberately made his way back to his lines he could hear Marcus alternating between laughing and shouting.

"Preserve the Republic! Aquila and Cicero. What a naive pair. People don't want freedom. They want riches, glory, and power! You are about to die, Aquila, and I will crucify Cicero for what he has said about me."

Marcus raised his arm and his cavalry charged across the open space, crashing into Aquila's lines. The shriek of the centurions' whistles penetrated above the din of the battle.

Aquila pulled himself back to survey the battle. He sent riders to the city gate to bring support from his third cavalry cohort, and sent scouts to determine the location of Marcus's infantry. The two mounted forces fought near the city walls with neither gaining a clear advantage. Marcus had sent riders to notify his infantry to come at a fast march. However, the messengers were intercepted by Aquila's scouts, and the infantry never received Marcus's orders. Aquila's third cohort arrived, forcing Marcus's troops to disengage.

Aquila collected his wounded, and led his men into the city. The gates of the city were secured, and Marcus's forces were not interfered with as they recovered their wounded and returned to their camp. After Aquila was sure his men had adequate medical treatment and supplies, he sought out Decimus Brutus, finding him at his headquarters. Aquila relayed what Marcus had said. Brutus praised him.

"You fought Marcus to a standstill and retreated without major losses, and avoided his infantry. I would say you succeeded."

Aquila sat silently. His dour expression puzzled Brutus.

"You should be celebrating your victory... actually two victories. The most important objective was to stop Plancus. Their forces are weakened and we can hold out for another month with our supplies in the city."

"I wanted Antonius Marcus. I should have killed him when I had the chance," Aquila stated.

"But you didn't let your emotions take precedence over the military goals, Aquila. You are usually very steady, according to what I've been told. That's one reason I wanted you as legate— you are disciplined in battle, a commander who sees the whole picture and does not let personal emotions affect his decisions, a defender of the republic."

"You of all people should talk about seeing the big picture, sir!" Aquila barked back. "If you had been paying attention, instead of sitting within the security of the city walls, we could have trapped his infantry as well. Marcus's other legions were occupied building their camp. You had two legions holed up in this stinking city. You could have destroyed their only mobilized legion and then followed up by attacking their unfinished camp. This campaign would be over! And Marcus might be dead."

Brutus was speechless. Aquila guzzled what remained of his wine and stomped out of the room.

Brutus had made his decision to stay inside the city, and Antonius Marcus in turn cut off Mutina and laid siege to the city. For weeks, Aquila recommended some sorties against the enemy as their adversary built fortified camps around the periphery of the city. Brutus refused to risk any troops.

He also declined to send out any scouts, fearing they would

be captured and reveal the strength inside the city. He reminded Aquila their only allies were across the Adriatic in Greece.

#

A Roman scout sent by Octavius arrived in Mutina in the fourth week of the siege. He addressed Brutus in his office.

"A battle has just ended ten miles south at Forum Gallorum. Antonius Marcus's forces intercepted and defeated Consul Pansa's legions. The consul was killed, but Octavius and his co-consul Hurtius arrived with reinforcements just as the battle ended. They forced Marcus's troops to retreat back to their fortified camps."

The messenger handed Brutus a sealed scroll from Octavius. He read the message:

"Let me remind you the senate has pardoned you and all the Liberatores. I have been appointed to assist Consul Hurtius in lifting the siege of Mutina. We will attack Marcus again in several days. Decimus, you should deliver a strong sortie from Mutina to force Marcus's legions to fight on two fronts." Legate of the Praetorian Guard—Caesar Octavius.

On the morning of April 21, C. Pansa and A. Hirtius COS, scouts from Consul Hurtius's legions slipped through Antonius Marcus's siege lines and arrived in Mutina to inform Decimus to join the attack. The legions of Hurtius and Octavius arrived from the south to break the siege around Mutina. Brutus refused to trust Octavius. He kept the message a secret and the gates of the city closed. By midmorning, Brutus's troops in Mutina detected the rumble of battle from the south. The Battle of Mutina had begun within sight of the city. Aquila entered Brutus's office.

"Sir, we must join this fight. Let me send out scouts to

determine what is happening."

"Aquila, we can't trust anyone now. The Republic has been dead for years. The most remote hope for a return to Roman tradition is for the Senate to take full control. That will not be possible with Octavius in command."

"But there has to be balance. What about the common people? No plebeian assemblies? No tribunes representing the people?"

Aquila stood waiting for a response. *Brutus has never really supported the Republic. He was a Senator from a very ancient patrician family and has used his alliance with the Liberatores only to assassinate Caesar.*

Brutus did not answer and Aquila stamped out of his office wearing a scowl. He returned to his quarters and paced the floor in frustration. He agonized over the last few weeks and the confusion of the civil war. *My former comrades are now enemies, and my old enemies are now allies. And I am being hunted as an assassin. Tullia is gone. This hollow, empty feeling...it is like there is a hole in my heart! But I still have a son! I must find a way to survive and return to him.*

But no, wait! Why did I not recognize her? Those beautiful green eyes! That was Tullia! The dark hair! Prisca always did look like Tullia's twin. Of course, she had to act the part! In order to protect her, Cicero must have circulated stories that Tullia died after childbirth! I am sure he sent them to Trebula. That is why he made that last offhand remark about Pontius Gaius!

Aquila exited the barracks and climbed to the parapets on the city wall to observe the battle. A group of officers approached him. Among them was the Primus Pilus, the senior

Centurion, who addressed Aquila.

"Legate, we heard of Brutus's decision. There are many of us ready to fight, especially if you lead us. This is the time to break the siege. Most of Marcus's men are engaged in fighting the Senate's legions."

"Centurion, I have already tried to convince Brutus to engage the enemy, but he would not consent. Gather the officers who want to fight and meet me at Brutus's office. Perhaps he will listen when he sees so many officers are in favor of joining the battle."

#

As the officers crowded into Brutus's office, Aquila let the Primus Pilus issue their appeal.

"I see Aquila has the widespread support of our officers to join in the battle against Antonius Marcus. I will agree to the foray if it is limited to one cohort of cavalry, no infantry is involved, and Aquila remains in Mutina," Brutus said.

The Primus Pilus glanced at Aquila, studied his officers, and answered for all of them, "Agreed."

Near the south gate of Mutina, Aquila helped organize the men and horses. A tribune expressed his concern.

"Aquila, only three hundred men have volunteered to go on the sortie. If you do not lead, we will not be able to recruit a full cohort. You must come with us now."

Aquila handed the tribune his helmet and red cloak.

"Wear these, mount my horse and assemble your men at the gate. More will follow you. Virtus!"

The battle had turned in favor of Hurtius and Octavius. As Antonius Marcus's legions were withdrawing to their fortified camp, the tribune bearing Aquila's helmet and cloak led his mounted cohort to cut off their retreat. He noticed a flash of red near the camp's gate and realized it was the cape of Antonius Marcus. As he charged to intercept him, the infantry guarding Marcus's camp let loose a flight of javelins. By all appearances, one of those killed by the missiles was Aquila.

Although Octavius's forces won the field, Marcus was able to flee with a large part of his army. Octavius's respect for the Roman legionaries on both sides of the Battle of Mutina compelled him to recover the fallen and ensure reverent handling of their remains. Among those bodies recovered and cremated with military honors were those identified as the Consul Hurtius and the Legate Lucius Pontius Aquila.

Now that both Pansa and Hurtius were dead, Rome was without consuls and Octavius assumed the command of the senatorial legions. From atop Mutina's wall, Brutus had watched his cavalry cohort be decimated by Marcus's infantry and had seen his cavalry commander go down, thinking it was Aquila. Decimus Brutus did not trust Octavius and led his army east to join his allies in Greece.

#

Aquila had slipped out of Mutina unnoticed as the cavalry exited the gate. He rode south along the Via Aemilia. His decision to flee continued to torment him during the long ride across Italy. A tumultuous back-and-forth battle roared through his mind. He put a decided stop to it when he shouted into the wind, "If this is desertion, then so be it! I am glad to abandon such a corrupt system! To hell with it all!"

Aquila rode until midnight. As the full moon reached its

zenith, he guided his mount across an empty field and entered a copse of trees. He awoke at sunrise. From his hideaway, he watched the passage of several cavalry detachments among the traffic on the road. He did not trust the Senate's proclamation that all of Caesar's assassins had been pardoned. Even if he was not recognized, he knew he would be questioned about his possession of an army-issued horse. For days Aquila made sporadic progress toward southern Italy by traveling at night.

On the morning of the tenth day after departing Mutina, Aquila arrived in Trebula. Cicero's household guards, surprised to see him, let him through the walled enclosure into the grounds. Aquila jumped off his horse and ran into the villa's peristylium. He saw the silhouette of a dark-haired woman as she sat in the garden cradling a baby. *Tullia and Marianus made it here safely!* Aquila drew close, but suddenly stopped as his eyes met hers.

"You aren't Tullia! I saw Tullia . . . But you were her in Rome, I mean . . . No, this can't be!"

His outburst frightened Prisca. Marianus began to cry. She was speechless at first. Then, "No. No, sir. I . . . I am confused. We heard you had been killed at Mutina!"

Aquila raised his arms and shouted, "I was sure you were Tullia! This can't be. I have lost Tullia! I have lost everything!"

Behind him he heard a joyous shout.

"Aquila? Aquila?!" Tullia ran to him, threw her arms around his neck and kissed him. They embraced and were still and silent for several minutes. The world was blocked out as tears of happiness flowed freely. Then Aquila looked into those same green eyes he had seen in Rome, framed by hair turning blond again as the light roots grew longer.

#

Octavius returned to Rome. Antonius Marcus crossed the Alps and raised new legions. Lepidus, a former legate of Caesar, retained the loyalty of the legions in Gaul. In October, Octavius, Lepidus, and Antonius Marcus created the Third Triumvirate, a three-man dictatorship, which ended the Republic forever.

In Rome, Cicero refused to abandon his convictions and attempted to organize an opposition. He wrote letters to provincial governors pleading for them to bring their legions home and give the Senate the protection they needed against the triumvirate. Octavius, Lepidus, and Antonius Marcus generated a proscription list which sentenced to death without trial the assassins of Caesar. It also included many of those who had aided them and even those who had approved of their deed. Those who had been proscribed could be killed on sight. Octavius fervently opposed Marcus's insistence that Cicero be added to the proscription list. Octavius addressed the Senate for hours and listed for them all that Cicero had achieved for Rome and the Roman people. He reminded them that Cicero had not participated in nor had even known of the plans to assassinate Caesar. His appeals were ignored.

#

Montanus rode south out of Rome along the Via Appia with his troop of gladiators now turned assassins. Lining both sides of the road were mausoleums and tombs containing the ashes of the deceased. Alongside many of the tombs, statues had been erected to honor departed nobles. Montanus and his men searched hiding places among the structures. They had been on Cicero's trail for months and conflicting thoughts filled Montanus once again.

It would be a strange fate for Cicero if we caught him here where he will eventually be buried. I am not surprised a man as widely known and recognizable as Cicero is so hard to find. People love him and refuse to reveal his location. And although my men want to torture and kill citizens they suspect know about Cicero, I will not allow it. I respect the man. But I have a job to do.

Antonius Marcus told me to execute Cicero without mercy as soon as I find him. Yet in private, Marcus's wife offered a bonus if I deliver Cicero to her alive. She wants revenge for Cicero's defamation of her husband.

Marcus deserved everything Cicero said about him. Marcus is the scoundrel, not Cicero. But I have a job to do.

When I was a gladiator, my very life depended on doing my job. It still does. Marcus told me not to return unless I kill Cicero.

Montanus was not certain what alerted him as they passed the litter on the road that afternoon. Perhaps it was because the entourage did not have a contingent of bodyguards or it could have been the fact the curtains were closed in the heat of the day. He stopped the carriers and demanded whoever was inside to show himself.

As soon as Cicero pulled back the curtains, several gladiators shouted, "It is Cicero! We have finally caught him."

Cicero addressed Montanus.

"There is nothing proper about what you are doing, soldier, but do try to kill me properly."

Montanus knew the reward would be substantial if he brought in Cicero alive. A slave and a gladiator most of his life, he had bought his freedom using funds saved from special awards during his successful career. He was now about to express the freedom of choice he had earned.

Cicero leaned out of the litter. When he looked into Montanus's eyes, he knew the man would honor him. Cicero bowed his head. Montanus's sword was efficient and merciful.

#

The hamlet of Cominium, hidden deep in the Apennine Mountains of southern Italy, had been founded hundreds of years earlier by Pontius Cominius, a Roman seeking freedom and refuge. The people of Cominium lived as self-reliant shepherds.

Marianus loved to help his father tend the sheep and goats in the high mountain meadow. The toddler swung his small shepherd's staff at the bugs and butterflies, as Lucius watched with pride.

Tullia called, "Marianus, Lucius, come eat!"

They ran eagerly across the meadow toward their home.

EPILOGUE

Peace was possible for the Roman world once Octavius's forces defeated the joint fleets of Antonius Marcus and Cleopatra at Actium. Rome, no longer a republic, became an empire ruled by one man. Cicero's son, Marcus Tullius Cicero Minor, assisted by Octavius in his election as Consul, experienced the satisfaction of announcing to the Senate the naval defeat of Antonius Marcus. Although Octavius had not been able to save Cicero, he was now in complete control and his deep remorse drove him to protect and support the statesman's family.

#

Aquilina, ignorant of these world events, had experienced a time of peace growing up in the Roman province of Pontus in the sixteen years following the Battle of Zela. And now, she considered today the happiest day of her life. Aquilina's parents had arranged for her to marry Jaffe, the young man she had always hoped would be her husband. She grasped her bulla that hung around her neck. It held the green garnet ring her mother Miriam had said was a gift from her father. Aquilina loved her stepfather, a Hebrew, who affectionately called her Ardi, but she had promised if she ever had a son, she would name him Aquila.

United States Constitution and the Roman Republic

The government of the United States is not based on the ancient Greek democracies. Instead, the founding fathers used the Roman Republic as a basis to form a representative government.

The hatred of a king was a commonality for the Americans in 1776 and the Romans of 505 BC. Both revolutions rejected the idea of one man holding power. Both governments created systems that elected representatives of executive, judicial, and legislative branches of government to maintain checks and balances of power.

In the Roman Republic, two consuls, instead of one president, were elected by popular vote and each had veto power over the other. The citizens also elected ten tribunes who directly represented the people. These tribunes could veto laws proposed by the Senate that might be harmful to the people they represented. Elections were held every year, which helped maintain the wishes of the people.

Roman citizens during the Republic had freedom of speech, right to trial, equality in the eyes of the law, and freedom to seek economic success. These were the same rights that Americans fought for in 1776. The Roman Republic lasted for five hundred years.

ABOUT THE AUTHOR

Since childhood, Mike Ponzio has read books on ancient Rome. He traded books and stories with his father, Joseph Ponzio, and they discussed the origins of the family surname. Mike traveled around the Mediterranean to Europe, Asia, and Africa, visiting many of the locations he would later write about. He continues to travel and writes stories which he imagines may have taken place during the lives of ancient ancestors.

Mike met his wife, Anne, in 1975 at a University of Florida karate class. Since that time both have taught Cuong Nhu Oriental Martial Arts. With John Burns, they wrote and published six instructional books on martial arts weapons. Mike retired in 2015, after working as an environmental engineer for thirty-seven years. Anne and Mike have raised four sons, who are all engineering graduates.

The novels listed below will join *Pontius Aquila: Eagle of the Republic* in the *Lover of the Sea* series. The title characters are historical.

- *Pontius Pilatus: Dark Passage to Heaven*

- *St. Pontius: Bishop of Rome*

For more information go to the author's website:
History & Historical Fiction: Pontius, Ponzio, Pons, and Ponce
https://mikemarianoponzio.wixsite.com/pontius-ponzio-pons

Pontius Aquila: Eagle of the Republic
Bibliography

1. "Ancient Roman Medicine." Ancient Roman Medicine. Accessed March 28, 2010. http://www.mariamilani.com/ancient_rome/Ancient_Roman_Medicine.htm.
2. Andrews, Robert, and Brown, Jules. *Sicily: The Rough Guide.* London: Rough Guides, 1996.
3. "Appian, The Mithridatic Wars." - Livius. Accessed March 28, 2010. http://www.livius.org/sources/content/appian/appian-the-mithridatic-wars/.
4. Benjamin, Sandra. *Sicily: Three Thousand Years of Human History.* Hanover, NH: Steerforth Press, 2006.
5. Bunson, Matthew. *A Dictionary of the Roman Empire.* New York: Oxford University Press, 1995.
6. Calverley, C. S., *Theocritus,* Cambridge: Deighton, Bell and Co.,London, Bell and Daldy, 1869.
7. "Dictionary of Greek and Roman Biography and Mythology/Nisus." Dictionary of Greek and Roman Biography and Mythology/Nisus - Wikisource, the free online library. Accessed July 27, 2010. https://en.wikisource.org/wiki/Dictionary_of_Greek_and_Roman_Biography_and_Mythology/Nisus.
8. Durant, Will. *The Life of Greece: Being a History of Greek Civilization.* New York: Simon and Schuster, 1939.
9. "Fragments of Book VIII." Cassius Dio 8. Accessed August 24, 2008. http://www.the-romans.eu/books/cassius-dio-8.php.
10. Grant, Michael, and Arthur Banks. *Ancient Atlas of History.* Dorset Press, 1971.
11. Hazel, John, *Who's Who In the Roman World,* Routledge, Taylor and Francis Group, London, 2000.
12. Heichelheim, Fritz M., and Cedric A. Yeo. *A History of the Roman People.* Englewood Cliffs, NJ: Prentice-Hall, 1962.
13. "Internet History Sourcebooks." Internet History Sourcebooks. Accessed January 27, 2014. http://sourcebooks.fordham.edu/halsall/ancient/suetonius-julius.asp.

14. Lewis, Jon E. *The Mammoth Book of Eyewitness Ancient Rome*. New York: Carroll & Graf Publishers, 2004.
15. Lewis, Naphtali and Reinhold, Meyer, ed., *Roman Civilization Source Book I The Republic*, New York, Harper and Row, 1951.
16. Lewis, Naphtali and Reinhold, Meyer, ed., *Roman Civilization Source Book II The Empire*, New York, Harper and Row, 1955.
17. "List of Ancient Romans." Wikipedia. Accessed September 1, 2009. https://en.wikipedia.org/wiki/List_of_ancient_Romans.
18. Long, George and Macleane, A.J. Reverend, eds., *Bibliotheca Classica, M. Tullii Ciceronis Orationes*, London, Whittaker and Co., 1858.
19. "Marriage." Marriage. Accessed September 1, 2009. http://www.roman-empire.net/society/soc-marriage.html.
20. Nelson, Eric, *The Complete Idiot's Guide to the Roman Empire*, Alpha Books and Pearson Education, Inc., 2001.
21. Plutarch, John Dryden, and Arthur Hugh Clough. *Plutarch's Lives of Illustrious Men. Corrected from the Greek and revised*. Boston: Little, Brown, 1876.
22. "Reading, Writing, Romans." Accessed January 8, 2017. http://www.ashmolean.org/ashwpress/latininscriptions/.
23. "Rome Exposed - Marriage and Customs and Roman Women." Accessed September 1, 2009. http://www.classicsunveiled.com/romel/html/marrcustwom.html.
24. Suetonius, Alexander Thomson, and Thomas Forester. *The Lives of the Twelve Caesars*. London: G. Bell and Sons, 1901.
25. "The Giant Triton." Giant Triton (Charonia tritonis). Accessed December 5, 2016. http://triton.yolasite.com/.
26. The Roman Republic: The Foundations of the United States Constitution, Brennan McKimmey-Yahoo Voices, Sources: Michael Grant's "History of Rome http://voices.yahoo.com/the-roman-republic-foundations-united-states-233726.html?cat=37

Made in the USA
Columbia, SC
28 April 2017